SEEKING REDEMPTION
Aidan & Ethan

CAMERON DANE

ISBN: 978-1461045403
SEEKING REDEMPTION: AIDAN AND ETHAN

Originally released in e-book format in December 2008 by Liquid Silver
Books

Manufactured in the USA
Cover Art by Anne Cain
Print Design and Formatting by April Martinez
Edited by Chrissie Henderson

PROLOGUE

Ethan threw himself down on the bank of the creek and looked up through the trees at a sky so blue it hurt his eyes to see it. He turned to his best friend sprawled out right next to him and whispered, "It's finally over."

The dark-haired young man sitting next to Ethan rolled onto his side and laid his head to rest on his hand. "Yep." Pale green eyes flashed with mirth, and a familiar grin hitched up at one corner, making Ethan's heart skitter. "Now we can do whatever the hell we want, wherever the hell we want to do it." He reached out, snagged the tasseled cap out of Ethan's hand and tossed it up in the air, catching it with barely a glance. "So, where do you want to go first?"

"I don't know." Ethan hadn't let himself think too far

beyond getting through high school. More than that, he hadn't let himself think that a cool guy like Aidan would still be friends with him by graduation. Well, they'd just done that earlier today, so it might be okay to start dreaming a little bit. "New York, California," he kicked Aidan's cowboy boot with his dress shoe, "Texas." Anything that would take them away from the little western Maine town, Redemption -- at least for a little while.

Aidan shot to his feet, hauling Ethan up with him. "Oh, so you want to learn to rope cattle with the cowboys, huh?" He whipped his graduation gown over his head and quickly twisted it into a rope. "Better start running, or I'm gonna give you your first lesson right here."

Snapping the material at Ethan like a wet towel in a gym locker room, Aidan gave a warning that cracked across the quiet of the late afternoon.

"Shit! What the hell!" Ethan took off through the woods, the blood rushing through his veins as the heat of Aidan reached him through the cool air, his friend hot on his trail. "No, no, no! I changed my mind. I don't want to rustle cattle anymore. Inbred cowboys, hanging around after work fucking barn animals. No, we'll go somewhere else."

"Now you're disrespecting where I come from!" Aidan's deep voice rang out, catching Ethan and sinking into his pores, as the teen's attempts to rope him with the graduation gown had yet to do. "You're gonna pay for that, Ashworth. I swear I'm gonna kick your ass."

"You have to catch me first, jackass!" Ethan shouted, feeling high as a kite just from being in Aidan's presence. It had been that way for two years now, ever since Ethan had stood up for Aidan outside the guy's job one Saturday afternoon. Aidan had given him a grudging thank you afterward, and slowly, very slowly, they had become inseparable.

"Maybe, Ash, but when I catch you," Aidan took a good swing at Ethan with the graduation gown, but Ethan ducked and swerved before it looped him over the head, "you're gonna remember that I'm bigger than you and will kick your ass!"

Ethan kept up his pace, stuffing down a moan at the reminder of Aidan's muscular physique. Damn it, he did not need to be thinking shit like that about his only friend. "Bigger makes you slower." He threw a glance over his shoulder as he taunted Aidan, and then wished he hadn't. One look away from his path and his graduation gown snagged a low tree branch, catching him up and slowing down his foot race. Ethan yanked open the snaps and scrambled to get out of the blue gown, doing a roll around the trunk of the massive tree to which his gown had become attached. Adrenaline rushing, he circled away, getting to the other side, away to safety … or so he thought. One arm still trapped in the gown, bent around the tree at an awkward angle, Ethan sucked in a breath as Aidan captured him from the other side.

"Ah-ha!" Triumph shone in Aidan's eyes, open in a way the young man rarely let anyone see. Aidan pressed the twisted length of material across Ethan's chest and pinned him to the tree with it, his hands on either side of Ethan's body. "Gotcha."

His chest rising and falling deeply with every breath he took, Ethan couldn't look away. Never wanted to whenever they were together. "Yeah." The sun twinkled high in the sky, breaking through the treetops with sharply-angled slashes of bright light. But the air around Ethan felt charged with electricity, as if Mother Nature prepared for a storm. "You got me."

"Yeah." Aidan's hold on the tree loosened and, along with the material, it fell to Ethan's waist. "I do, don't I." He let go of the wrinkled gown entirely and leaned in, entwining his fingers with Ethan's free hand as he did. "Shit," Aidan muttered, "I knew you felt it too."

"Yeah." The confession slipped out before Ethan could call it back.

"Yeah, I thought so." Closing the small distance between them, Aidan cursed one more time. "Hoped so," he added roughly, and then sealed his lips to Ethan's, crushing him with a hard kiss.

Elation whipped through Ethan as everything he'd ever wanted burst to life right in front of him, against him, in him, as Aidan squeezed their hands together and forced his way inside Ethan's mouth, deepening the kiss. Ethan gave into the moan he'd wanted to let escape just a few minutes ago and moved into Aidan's space, rubbing himself all up against the hard length of the other boy, drawing a mutual trembling of bodies from the young men. Ethan finally managed to free his other arm from his gown and immediately found Aidan's hand, locking on tight.

Aidan broke the kiss, but stayed close. Moist breath fanned Ethan's lips, and Aidan's mossy gaze didn't waver. "More, please. Give me more." Aidan's voice was thick and insistent. He shoved their linked hands in between their bodies and somehow got them each working on the belt of the other. "I want to touch you." With buttons quickly undone, their zippers whispered through the afternoon breeze, and it was as if no animal dared move around them and make a sound. "Wanna make you come."

"Oh fuck." Ethan shuddered. "Me too." They pushed Aidan's jeans, and Ethan's dress pants, and then both of their underwear, down past their hips. Hard cocks sprang free, quickly wrapped up and squished together by two pairs of eager hands. Ethan gasped, his lips parting as Aidan touched his dick -- a fantasy Ethan had awoken from many a wet dream from almost the moment they met. Looking down, he watched himself rub his hand down the velvety-hard length of Aidan's prick, groaning when he grazed his fingers over the tip and came away with fat beads of precum. Ethan leaked a thick line of pre-ejaculate too, and when Aidan pressed the center of his palm against the head of Ethan's penis, Ethan almost came right then. This was what he had wanted since spotting Aidan in the parking lot of their school during sophomore year, when all of his vague, abstract thoughts about kissing other boys coalesced and focused on one real person: Aidan.

Ethan entwined his fingers with Aidan's around their

cocks, and they jerked each other off in tandem with a rough handling, sometimes enough to make both of them wince. Ethan didn't dare back off or pull away, though, not for one second. Gritting his teeth against the insane pleasure of another boy touching him, of *this boy* touching him, Ethan glanced up at the hard lines of Aidan's face that at eighteen had already become someone who looked and felt like a man. Ethan's heart lurched dangerously, and he had no power or ability to censor himself.

"I love you, Aidan," he blurted, his voice husky with emotion. "Wanna be with you forever."

Aidan's eyes seemed to sharpen and clear, and his stare pierced right through to Ethan's soul. He strung a line of familiar foul words together and shook his head. "Fuck. I love you too, man." Then he slammed Ethan back into the tree with his weight and fused their mouths together in a violent kiss. He bit at Ethan's lips, and at the same time he yanked their hands with tight drags up and down their lined-up cocks.

"Together." Aidan made the one word sound like a command. "You and me." Their hands turned frantic around their dicks, and neither man could keep his hips from pumping for more.

Ethan looked right into Aidan's eyes, somehow clear in the blur of closeness. "Forever."

Aidan nodded, his lips scraping roughly over Ethan's. "Forever."

Ethan's entire body jerked and seized, and just like that, he started coming, shooting seed against Aidan in a thick film of cum. As soon as the first jet of liquid hit Aidan's skin, Aidan spurted too, hitting Ethan with the repeated, warm splashes of his orgasm. Ethan reveled in the feel of it. His balls already began tingling and recharging to go at it again as he imaged what it might be like to make Aidan come using his mouth … or something else. Ethan shivered just thinking about it.

Goddamnit, he was in love. Even better, the coolest guy in the whole fucking world loved him back. Ethan didn't think he could get any luckier than that.

And then, he did.

"I wasn't kidding all this time, you know," Aidan began. He let up his lock hold on Ethan's hand and released their dicks. He stuffed his cock back in his underwear and jeans -- God, Ethan loved that Aidan had worn jeans to graduation -- but he didn't zip or snap himself closed.

Ethan quickly did the same. "K-kidding about what?" Heat suffused Ethan's cheeks at his fumbling.

Aidan snatched his gown off the ground and unhooked Ethan's from the tree bark. Tossing them over his shoulder, he started back in the direction from which they had come. "About traveling with you for a few years," he said. Ethan hurried to Aidan's side and kept up with the taller boy's pace. "We can take everything we've saved," they'd both worked steady jobs through high school, "and just get the hell out for a little while." He glanced at Ethan out of the corner of his eye. "What do you think?"

Ethan didn't think his feet touched the ground. "I think," he pulled his shirt off over his head, smiling with new power when Aidan's focus openly fell to his bare chest, "we take a swim in the creek and make a plan!" He tackled Aidan around the waist. To the shouts and protests of the other young man, Ethan sent them both tumbling into the frigid water.

———

ETHAN COULDN'T KEEP THE SMILE off his face the next morning as he practically skipped up the front porch to Aidan's house and gave a sharp, happy rap to the red painted front door.

Aidan's younger brother Dev answered his knock.

"Oh, hey," Dev said, his voice cracking well beyond that of a normal twelve-year-old adolescent.

"Hey." Ethan decided to overlook the moisture brimming in Dev's eyes. He was probably in trouble, and the kid wouldn't want an older boy noticing and commenting. "Can I come in? I'm here to see Aidan."

"You won't find him here."

"What?" Icy fingers ran down Ethan's back. He stooped down, getting a better look at the tears in Devlin's eyes. "What's the matter? What's going on?"

Devlin's voice broke pitifully, but he shared.

With only a note left on the kitchen table that said he had to leave and not to worry about him or try to find him, Aidan was gone.

CHAPTER ONE

Back in Redemption to start a new chapter in his life, after all this time.

Damn.

Aidan Morgan leaned back in his chair in his new office, his heart already starting to pound in double-time as he imagined the meeting that would take place in just a few minutes. He would officially take over as chief of the fire department in a week, but his predecessor had already moved his stuff out of the building, happy to be retiring after twenty years in the local department. Soon to be moving to Florida, Chief Roger Robbins would introduce Aidan to his staff and volunteer crew in just a few minutes, but that was only part of the reason Aidan's hands trembled against the arms of his chair. Cursing, he dug his fingers into the worn leather covering and assured himself everything would be fine.

You came back for three reasons, he lectured himself, *and two of them just happen to be in your employ.*

Aidan had come home for his siblings and, as luck would have it, Devlin was one of his paid firefighters. A probie. His sister Maddie was a senior in high school, but already working part-time for a mechanic and nearly earning her own keep. Aidan had plans later on this afternoon to meet everyone at said auto shop and make sure they respected his baby sister. Dev and Maddie were powerful reasons for Aidan to want to come home to stay. He had one other though.

Ethan Ashworth.

Christ, Aidan's chest constricted just thinking the man's name. Over a dozen years away hadn't changed his reaction one bit. Aidan still wanted his best friend with an ache that defied sense. He remembered dark blond hair that had a tendency to get flyaway wings behind the ears when he let it go too long without a cut. He could still feel the lean, long torso, sparse of hair, hard shoulders, and strong arms that had defined cuts, but no bulk. Fuck, he couldn't forget the hard heat of Ethan's cock either. When Aidan closed his eyes he swore he could still feel the shape, length, and the smoothness of the cap over the head against his palm. Damn, he remembered all of that with vivid clarity.

What Aidan couldn't get out of his mind more than anything else, though, no matter how hard he tried, were Ethan's eyes, so blue they almost looked like royal purple sometimes. Whenever Aidan closed his eyes Ethan's gaze haunted him -- from the dark defiance in it on the day he'd stepped to Aidan's side when some asshole rich kids had harassed him outside his work, to that day against the tree when Ethan's eyes became such a smooth, pure blue Aidan swore he couldn't see a single inflection in the color. Then, although he hadn't seen it in person, in Aidan's head, he watched that blue turn to the colors of a storm the moment Ethan found out that Aidan had walked away and left him alone. Fuck, the thought of that killed Aidan a thousand times over, virtually every day.

A sharp stab hit Aidan in the stomach. His gut twisted as he thought about which eyes he would see when he came face to face with Ethan again.

Rap, rap, rap. Aidan snapped out of his memories as whoever knocked on his door didn't wait for an invitation, but merely pushed his way inside. Chief Robbins, still fit and barrel-chested, leaned the heel of his hand against the doorjamb and put his focus on Aidan. "You look good there, son," he said. "Like the office and job was made for you."

"Thanks." Aidan would have to see if the job still *looked* like him when the town found out why he'd come home. "I'm anxious to get started."

"Well, that's why I'm here." A hint of the chief's southern upbringing still tinged his voice, mixing in with the northeastern drawl he'd been living among for most of his adult life. "Everyone has arrived. You ready to do this?"

No time like the present to get the first meeting out of the way. "Yep." Aidan's hands went clammy, joining in on the racing of his heart. "Let's do it."

Ethan would be among the group of volunteer firefighters mingling right outside this building, and Aidan couldn't wait to see the man he had become.

———

"SON OF A BITCH." ETHAN nursed his second beer while staring at the TV, although for the life of him he could not give an answer if asked what was on. He hadn't been aware of much of anything other than a boiling heat that sat just under his skin since hearing of the chief's announcement about the firehouse's new boss one week ago. Chief Robbins officially shared with his crew that he would be retiring from the job, and that a familiar face would take over the position.

Goddamn fucking son of a bitch. Aidan Morgan was the new goddamn fucking chief of the fire department where Ethan just happened to volunteer. Why? Why would the man do this to Ethan? Why would he come home after all this time, without even having the respect to call Ethan and let him in on the move?

Ethan snorted and took another swig of his beer. "Why the hell would he tell me?" he said, waving his hand at his audience. His dog Ozzie raised his brows and looked around the room of the open cabin, as if asking, "You talking to me?"

The boxer settled into the couch across from the recliner

where Ethan sat, looking like he was willing to lend his floppy ears to the discussion. "It's not like he ever bothered to leave me a note when he left, or *ever* tried to get in touch with me, even once," Ethan shared with the dog. "Why should I think that he'd warn me so that I wasn't humiliated when I walked into the station and found him standing there waiting to introduce himself to the group. *As my boss.*" The dog lifted his head and gave a little growl, making Ethan smile for the first time in seven days. "Thank you, Oz. I knew you'd be on my side."

It didn't matter that Ethan would only be humiliated on the inside. It was not as if anyone knew what had happened in the woods that day so many years ago, or of the plans he and Aidan had made on the mountain that day. Still, Aidan would know. One look into his eyes and Ethan was terrified Aidan would be able to see the longing still living inside him. The embarrassing, stupid, ridiculous *wanting* for a man who'd left him thirteen years ago without a word and had broken Ethan's young, idiot heart.

What killed Ethan more than anything was that Aidan had never called to explain or check in, even just to see how Ethan was doing. Aidan had never given Devlin any messages for Ethan over the years either, and had never asked Devlin how Ethan was getting along. Ethan knew, because one day not long after Aidan had disappeared, he'd needed Aidan like he'd never needed anyone before, and so had cornered Dev and asked him if Aidan wanted an update about Ethan, or if he had a new phone number where old friends could give him a call.

Dev had just said that his big brother seemed happy in his new life, and that he never asked about Redemption, or any of the people still living here.

Hot anger burned Ethan's cheeks at the memory, something he thought he had put behind him long ago. That was before last week.

Before Ethan found out that Aidan Morgan was coming home.

———

AIDAN GRITTED HIS TEETH AS his truck bumped along the rocky road, pissed as hell that he might kill the shocks on his brand new vehicle before the ink on the paperwork had a chance to dry. Some things just couldn't be helped though. And some things couldn't be put off. Thirteen years apart was long enough.

The line of trees and scenery pulled Aidan's focus away from the slice of hurt he hadn't been able to hide from his crew at his introduction meeting earlier as he'd looked down the line of men and one woman and didn't find the only face he wanted to see.

Ethan. Christ, that had some sting to it. Ethan had delivered a cold, hard rejection, even if Aidan was the only one who knew it. So very different from the day he'd first met Ethan Ashworth, and how it had forever changed his life...

———

…Aidan wiped down the outdoor table and counted to ten under his breath, doing his best to control the heat rising under his skin, threatening to push his anger out from hiding.

No, no. Ignore it, Morgan. Just do your job and pretend you don't hear anything. You can't afford to get into trouble here. Just keep it cool.

"Probably should pants him and make sure he doesn't have a pussy," a kid taunted from one of the other tables outside the fast food joint. The three other guys with the teen laughed and egged their buddy on. "Ain't no other guy I know who would turn down a shot at the football team and a date with Kim Donner. I bet he never got in trouble in Texas at all." The teen brought up Aidan's recent past -- something no one in this town should know. "Bet Mommy and Daddy had to move him away after everyone found out their son is really their daughter."

Aidan bit down the retort he itched to shoot off, and he curled his fist around the damp cloth in his hand so that he didn't rush the other table and start a fight. *Think about Maddie and Devlin*, Aidan reminded himself, for the tenth time in ten minutes. *One more slip up and you're gone. You'll be out of their lives for good.*

School and work, work and school … that was Aidan's life now. The life he'd agreed to live, without incident. It had been this or juvenile detention back in Texas, where he would have lost any relationship with his brother and sister for good.

With renewed pictures of his siblings in his head, Aidan

finished wiping down the last table. The harassment from his classmates went on the whole time, degenerating into name-calling and foul language well beyond calling him a girl. Aidan thanked God nobody else was outside to hear the slurs and get offended enough to complain. *Goddamn jerks.* Aidan couldn't afford to lose his job. And he just knew he would too. No one was going to reprimand three guys from the high school football team, as well as the junior class president. No, Aidan -- the kid with the arrests in Texas -- *that nobody here was supposed to know about* -- would be the one cited for causing trouble, and he damn well knew it. He couldn't outrun his choices, and it was stupid of him to think he could start a new life here in Redemption.

Shit, even the name of the town mocked him.

He would try though. Like he'd been doing for six months, he'd keep his head down and his nose clean. For his brother and his sister, Aidan would give this move everything he had in him. Even if it meant ignoring a table full of privileged fuckers who each deserved a fist to the face and a boot in their ass.

Aidan growled at the injustice, but kept it under his breath. He threw the damp cloth over his shoulder and moved to the trashcan, removing the lid so he could empty it and put in a new lining. As he tied the full bag closed, he looked up and found a pair of blue eyes watching him from inside The Burger Joint. The guy quickly turned his blond head down and broke contact, but their gazes had connected long enough to shake fear through Aidan. In that moment, Aidan had been unguarded, with all the anger, frustration, and yeah, self-pity, those other bastards had churned up in him showing as clear as day in his eyes. Aidan didn't let anybody see him like that. Nobody could know he *cared*, and get the upper hand.

Shaking off the discomfort of exposure, Aidan quickly put a new bag in the trashcan, put the lid back on, and hauled the full bag around the corner of the building to the dumpster. He put his arm over his nose as the stench grew, quickly tossing the bag and closing the top, and then crammed the full container closed. Afterward, he moved the locking bar back over the top to hold the cover down.

With that truly crappy task done, Aidan turned, prepared to go on to his next crappy assignment … and quickly found himself cornered by the four dudes who'd been harassing him out front.

"Maybe you didn't hear us before." The big talker, Keith, Aidan thought that was his name, stepped forward, very nearly getting into Aidan's space. "So are you deaf too, Texas?" This one particular jackass liked to harp on where Aidan used to live, for some reason. "Are you a deaf, dumb, *chick*, Texas?" He shoved Aidan in the shoulder, pushing him against the wall. "You want to show us your pussy?"

Aidan's head hit the brick, and his fighting instincts fought to break free. "Back the fuck off, right now," he uttered, his lips barely moving. "Don't touch me again."

"Oh, you gonna make me?" Keith stretched out his arms and leaned in, looking like some preppy wanna-be gangster. "A pretty little girl like you? All by yourself?"

"Not all by himself." A deep, surprisingly hard voice cut across the alley, spinning Aidan's attackers in its direction. It was the blond guy who'd caught Aidan unaware a moment ago. *Shit.* This wasn't going to end well. "He has at least one person to help even the odds. I've taken five years of Tae-Kwon-Do, and I'm about a month away from getting my black belt." The dude moved closer and pointed at Aidan. "I keep hearing rumors about the things this guy did in Texas that got him fucking kicked out of the state. So I guess you have to ask yourselves, do you feel good about your chances? Right here? Right now?"

Keith pushed in with a menacing step, and Aidan moved in to protect his protector.

"What the hell do you think you're doing, E --" *Whio, whio, whio, whio.* Keith stopped cold.

Sirens filled the air, freezing everyone in place.

"Oh," the blond kid slipped his cell phone out of his pocket and held it up, "I called the cops too. I don't think the three of you want to get in trouble and benched over this." His focus moved to the tall, skinny boy standing back a bit from the other three jerks. "And, Carl, I don't know, the school board might not like that their junior class president is getting in trouble with the law." Aidan's impromptu champion cupped his ear. "Sounds like they're getting closer." The guy's voice reeked with confidence. "You take off, and I'll probably just tell them that I made a mistake, and *didn't* see four guys about to beat up on one." He turned to Aidan. "How about you?"

Aidan slid a hard gaze from this *stupidly* brave classmate to the other four. "Nothing happened here. I'm just doing my job."

"Good," Keith said. He pointed right in Aidan's face, but he did quickly back up. "Keep it that way. Or I might just come back."

Aidan didn't so much as flinch. He held his breath, though, and didn't take his focus off Keith and his buddies until they disappeared from sight. A full minute went by where both remaining boys stood in silence, watching the alley, as if waiting for the others to come back.

Finally, the blond boy slumped against the wall and let out a long breath. He rolled his head against the bricks and looked Aidan dead-on in the eyes. "Ethan Ashworth." He stuck out his hand. "Nice to meet you."

Aidan hesitated, uncertain. What was this guy's deal? Nobody stepped in and made themselves a target like he'd just done, without wanting something in return. Aidan didn't need to owe someone a favor. When collected, those things tended to get expensive and complicate a life, when all Aidan wanted and needed right now was simple and clean.

Which didn't include law enforcement.

Shit.

"You shouldn't have called the cops," he said, already trying to work an explanation out in his head that would convince his mother and father he hadn't started any trouble.

"Oh." Ethan smiled. His cheeks went red, and Aidan's breath caught at the sight. "I didn't call them. That was just an amazing coincidence. I thought fast on my feet. There aren't any cops coming here." Ethan's face sobered as quickly as it had lit up. "You don't have to worry."

"Thanks." Guilt warred with gratitude inside Aidan, and he didn't know how to deal with either one. Obviously this Ethan guy had heard the rumors about his trouble in Texas, or else he wouldn't have said what he did. Defensiveness and self-preservation were familiar ground for Aidan, and he slipped into the cloak as naturally as breathing. "You shouldn't have made yourself a target though. Now they're gonna mess with you too."

"Won't be anything new." Ethan shoved his hands into his pockets, his shoulders dipping in a slouch. "Sometimes you have to stand up though. I made the choice, and I'll live with it. Well, anyway," he started walking backward, "I'll let you get back to work." As in the restaurant when caught staring, Ethan dropped his stare and looked away. "See you around school."

Ethan moved down the alley, and Aidan couldn't explain it, but he started to run.

"Ethan!" he shouted, racing to grab the guy's arm and spin him around.

When Ethan looked up Aidan found himself looking into those blue eyes again, and he didn't know what in the hell to say. He hadn't been a friend to anybody in such a long time that he didn't even know how to be just an acquaintance. And he really didn't know how to accept someone helping him for no other reason than it was the right thing to do.

"Thanks," he finally said again, stupidly. "Even though you really didn't have to do it." *Crap, that was ungrateful and dumb.* "But thanks anyway." Aidan jammed his hand in Ethan's direction before he thought twice and changed his mind. "My name is Aidan Morgan, by the way."

"Good to meet you, Aidan." Ethan slipped his hand into Aidan's and shook it. The contact shocked Aidan. The size of Ethan's hand, its warmth, and the hard calluses that matched Aidan's rocked a small tremor through Aidan's system.

Uncomfortable with the strange awareness, Aidan yanked his hand away. "Okay," he mumbled. "Bye."

"Listen." The sharp tone of Ethan's voice grabbed Aidan's attention. "Maybe you don't want to do it, and maybe you don't really care, but I eat lunch by myself pretty much every day. That's when guys like Keith find it easiest to make a person a target. If you want, if you don't already eat with somebody, maybe we can eat together." He slipped his hands into his pockets again, shrugging. "Strength in numbers, you know?"

Aidan stood there, mute. He ate alone at school too. He did it on purpose though. If he didn't push his way into any of the established crowds then he wouldn't have to worry about making the wrong choice again. He would stay out of trouble.

"Well, think about it." Ethan stepped back, as if he sensed Aidan needed some space. "I sit at the bench outside the science building, should you ever want to find me." He smiled, sort of lopsided, and lifted his hand in a small wave. "See ya."

"Yeah." Aidan pushed his hands into the pockets of his jeans, and turned back to the entrance of The Burger Joint. "Bye."

Aidan put his head down and got back to work, but the only thing he could think of for the next three hours of his shift, and then all night when he went home, was whether he could take a chance and let Ethan Ashworth in...

———

...Aidan jerked out of the memory as he got closer to his destination, but once again the surrounding dense forest area washed over him with familiarity. Much as he tried to fight the onslaught of memories, they overtook him and he slipped back in time again, to the day he'd decided to let Ethan behind the wall of his defenses and move him from lunch-mate to real friend...

———

...Aidan turned in a circle, his breath almost stolen away as he took in the massive trees, and the trickling creek, and the absolute stillness and silence all around him. A chill went through him, and he quickly glanced over at Ethan. He breathed a silent sigh of relief when he only got the blond guy's back. Aidan didn't need people staring or trying to get too close.

Or trying to get him in trouble.

"You sure we're not trespassing on private property?" Aidan's voice cut through the quiet. From ten feet away Ethan jumped and spun around. Ethan's eyes, so blue and weirdly piercing, made Aidan's stomach feel funny. Aidan quickly looked down at the lichen-covered ground. "I don't give a shit or anything." Roughness in Aidan's voice covered his nerves. "I just want to know so I can be ready to run, if I have to."

"You may not have to care about getting in trouble, but I do," Ethan replied, drawing Aidan's attention back up to him. His hands buried in the front pockets of his jeans, Ethan shrugged while his entire face turned crimson. "I know you must have noticed by now that I don't do a lot of partying like most of the other kids at school. Let me tell you, there's a damn good reason for that. I don't have any interest in getting in trouble or caught drinking, or spending the night in jail, and then having my dad send me off to military school. And he would, I know it. So you don't have to worry that I'm gonna take you somewhere we shouldn't be. Believe me, no one cares that we're here."

"Okay," Aidan mumbled. Some of the contrasts Aidan had noticed in Ethan suddenly started to fall into place. "So that's why you don't really look like a nerd or anything, but you kind of act like one." Aidan's entire body immediately heated. "Oh, hey, man, I'm sorry." *Shit. What the hell?* Aidan didn't let his private thoughts slip out to just anyone. Not like that. "I wasn't trying to knock you or be mean."

A little smile tugged the corner of Ethan's mouth. "It's okay. I might act like a geek, but least I don't look like one."

The small smile from Ethan turned into a full-out grin, and Aidan stuffed his hands into his pockets so that he didn't reach out and touch. Jesus, he'd already been dreaming about touching Ethan. Too much.

"I guess that's something," Ethan added sheepishly, "huh?"

"Yeah," Aidan said. "I see a lot of girls looking at you, and I hear some talking about you too." *Girls. Yes, they were always good.* "You hang out a lot with them? You got a girlfriend?"

"I go out sometimes, but I don't really have a girlfriend." Ethan sat down on the ground and leaned back against the trunk of one of the massive trees. Listening as Ethan talked, Aidan did the same, so that they were sitting across from each other with some ten feet of space between them. "Like I said," Ethan continued, "I don't have any interest in going to military school. A girlfriend wouldn't necessarily make that happen, but the going out to parties with the girlfriend, and all of the hanging out that messes up the grades -- when I already have to try really hard just to get Bs and Cs -- would probably get me in trouble in other ways really fast. It's not worth it to me. That doesn't leave me with a lot of friends." The blush crept back over Ethan's cheeks. "But then again, if I were sent away for getting in trouble, it's not like I would see them anyway, if I had them. That's how I look at it."

"You're smart." Aidan spilled the words without thinking, lulled by this kid's honesty. He didn't seem to care what anyone else thought of him, and Aidan was lonely as hell for a friend. One who was strong enough to withstand peer pressure. "I wasn't. That's why we moved here. Because of me. Because I wasn't smart, like you are." The confessions just kept coming, and Aidan couldn't make them stop. He wanted Ethan to know the truth about his trouble in Texas, amidst all the rumors floating around school. "I was about one more stupid-ass stunt away from going into JD, screwing up the rest of my life, and probably losing my little brother and sister forever. The company my mom worked for offered her a really good job up here. My dad decided to quit his job and move the whole family here in order to get me away from my old friends. I have one shot to make my life right. I get in trouble up here, and I'm out for good. No more chances. They'll turn me over to the system, and say I was too hard to control. I don't want to lose my brother and sister. That's all I care about, so I'm not making any more mistakes."

Ethan shook his head and just started laughing. "Dude," he picked up a pinecone and tossed it at Aidan, "I think you met the one guy in school where staying out of trouble isn't going to be a problem." Aidan caught the makeshift ball and threw it back. He settled in, the knots in his stomach dissipating for the first time since moving to Redemption. Ethan sent the cone flying Aidan's way again, and as they played a casual game of catch, Ethan just started talking. "Let me tell you how hardcore my dad and his family are about keeping your nose clean. My cousin got in trouble last year, one time…"

...Aidan let the balm of that special day in his young life slip away as the cabin came into view. Right where he knew it would be. With a steepled roof and big, tall windows on either side of the door, the small home had a lovely porch that stretched the length of the front, and a set of steps in the middle that led right from the rocky path up to the front door.

Easing the truck to a stop, Aidan cut the engine and pocketed the keys, his blood simmering again as he pictured the man living inside this cabin. Along with that thought came the absence of said man at his mandatory meeting earlier today, and the simmer in Aidan quickly built into something infinitely hotter.

Aidan took the steps two at a time, taking just a moment to admire the bright red and yellow flowers in big terra cotta pots on either side of the landing. He forewent the doorbell and banged his fist against the solid wood of the front door. A dog started barking immediately, and that momentarily trapped Aidan in place. *He has a pet.* Huh. Fuck, that was sweet, and something Aidan hadn't ever allowed himself to imagine when dreaming about Ethan Ashworth.

"Oz, pipe down." A deep voice broke through the thickness of the front door, familiar, but different. More mature. Rougher. *Sexier.* Fuck again. Aidan's cock twitched, and the hairs on the back of his neck stood on end. Then the door opened.

Hair an even darker shade of blond than Aidan remembered, tan skin, sinewy muscles defined under a snug white T-shirt, and six feet of height that suddenly seemed much bigger than

Aidan recalled, filled the doorway. But those eyes. Christ, those blue eyes were exactly the same. Except, thirteen years later, they didn't twinkle with laughter or love. They didn't look a damn bit surprised to see him either.

Aidan's blood flowed again, and went from a simmer to an inferno.

"What the hell do you think you're doing?" Aidan barked, emotions from years of desire denied getting the better of him. "Not showing up for a mandatory meeting? You don't get to walk away from my crew just because we have some unfinished history, Ash. Not even close."

CHAPTER TWO

H *oly fuck.* Aidan Morgan. At his front door. Ethan worked like the very devil to school his features and not show any emotion whatsoever. He also willed his legs to lock so that he didn't stumble like a fool.

But ... *holy fuck.* No longer that forever-eighteen boy of Ethan's dreams, Aidan stood before him all man. All steely ropes of muscle beneath the white shirt with the Redemption fire department logo over his heart, to the black pants that didn't stop Ethan from picturing thighs and calves honed to hard perfection... *Shit.* The picture filled Ethan like a visual feast. He knew from the meeting with Chief Robbins that Aidan had been a firefighter in Arizona during the years he'd been away: God, how it showed in his stunning physique.

Ethan suddenly stood up straighter as the reality of that miniscule amount of information hit him. Ethan might know that one basic thing about Aidan, but he had nothing else.

Because Aidan had run.

What was it the jackass had said a minute ago? Something about not being able to leave his crew? *Bastard.*

"You wasted your money on gas driving up here, Chief." He met the man's sage-green gaze, and absolutely didn't waver. "In case you didn't read the roster, I'm on the *volunteer* crew, so you don't have any say in whether I stay or leave. I didn't miss the meeting today. I told Chief Robbins that I'd helped out for as long as I could, but that it was time for me to let it go."

The stubbly square jaw before him ticked visibly. "I know. He told me." Aidan leaned in and braced his hand against doorjamb, forcing Ethan to take an automatic step back.

Fucker. Trying to intimidate me. Ethan arched a brow and prayed the pounding in his chest didn't show on the outside. "Well, then there's your answer."

Aidan's pale eyes darkened and burned hot enough to start a fire of his own. "Do you think for one second I believe it's just a coincidence that you're walking away from the department, *now*, when you've been doing the work so successfully for five years?" Ethan paled at those words. "Oh yeah," Aidan didn't miss a beat, "I asked Roger how long you'd been volunteering, and he told me. I understand that you might still be a little angry with me --"

"Angry?" Ethan whispered the word with deathly softness.

Any of his kids down at the high school would know they had just stepped over Mr. Ashworth's line, and were probably about two seconds away from getting a serious amount of detention, or getting kicked right off the volleyball team. Right now, Ethan just barely checked throwing a punch at the man getting much too close to invading his personal space. "No, Aidan, I was *angry* twelve years ago." No way did this guy get to think he wouldn't have to address the damage he had done by leaving. "That came *after* the year of crushing hurt and humiliation I felt when your little brother had to tell me -- your *best* friend -- that you'd disappeared in the middle of the night to start a new life. Angry was how I felt then. Now I just think you were a liar and didn't deserve a second of the time I ever spent thinking about you." Ethan looked Aidan up and down, and he didn't feel the slightest urge to fuck him. He wanted to throw a punch at his mouth. *No, he's not worth the sore hand.* "I think that's about all I need to say. Goodbye." Ethan moved to slam the door.

Aidan caught it with the flat of his palm before it closed. "Okay, so you're not willing to hear me out right now; I get that."

"That implies there will be a day when I'll want to listen to you."

"All right, fine." Aidan's hard jaw ticked some more, drawing Ethan's eye. Ethan didn't remember this man having such a dead giveaway for his emotions, as the clenching of his jaw line conveyed.

He's pissed. Ethan barely covered his smirk. *Good.*

Aidan's mouth narrowed to hard line. His gaze flashed too, but then he retracted and said, "Putting aside for the moment that things ended badly between us, as the new chief of the RCFD I need qualified people on my crew. You know how few guys I have on the paid staff."

Ethan did know. Aidan would have an assistant chief, and seven full-time firefighters. The other ten people who staffed the house did so as part of the volunteer program.

"I can't afford to lose you," Aidan said. "At least not until I recruit some more folks who are willing to go through the training and join the group. Give me some time, Ash."

"Don't call me that." Only Aidan ever called Ethan that name. It had been special, once upon a time.

"Ethan, then." Aidan let go of the door and pushed his fingers through his dark hair, leaving unruly tunnels in their wake. "Come back to the firehouse until I get someone through the training who looks like they're gonna stick."

"You know that could take a long time." In Maine, volunteer firefighters had to go through the exact same training program as the paid crew, and then had to participate in a predetermined number of hours in training seminars and meetings in order to remain qualified for the work. In Redemption, most of the volunteers also gave of their time and took overnight shifts at the station alongside one or two of the paid men, depending upon the schedule. "People drop out left and right when they realize the commitment involved."

"I know," Aidan' replied. "Which is why I need you, man. The station needs more people, even if you weren't choosing to leave. I can't afford to have you go before I have at least one person to replace you." Aidan took a few more steps backward, allowing Ethan to breathe a little easier. Crossing his thick arms against his chest, Aidan scanned the length of Ethan's cabin. "Right now, no one knows you gave Roger your resignation. I told him to hold off and give me a chance to change your mind. It won't be a big deal for you to come back into the group for a while. You can start dropping hints that it's taking up too much of your time; that it's cutting into your time with a significant other…" His gaze came back to Ethan, the unspoken question in his eyes.

"You get nothing from me about my personal life, Aidan." Ethan's chest squeezed, and the words came out tight. "Not anymore."

"Fair enough." Aidan dipped his head. "That's your call. Have you made a decision about the volunteering? Can I count on you as part of my crew?"

Guilt over the town his family had called home for four generations nagged Ethan's conscience, and it shouted above the hurt still twisting, not so deeply buried anymore, for this one man.

"All right, fine," Ethan muttered. "I'll be there. I'll stay until you get a new recruit."

"One who sticks."

"Yes, one who lasts more than a month," Ethan conceded.

"But that's all you get."

"That's all I need." Aidan unhooked a pair of sunglasses from his belt loop, and then loped down the stairs. With the space now free, Ethan finally moved onto the porch and leaned his hip against the post at the top of the steps.

Pausing by his truck, Aidan turned, a small smile lifting the edge of his lips. Ethan closed his eyes for a moment as the feel of those lips clinging to his washed over him, spiking a desire to explore again and see how they had changed.

"All right then." Aidan broke the small silence. Ethan opened his eyes, finding Aidan's stare. "Let me get going. I have a ton of things that need doing before the job takes me over next week." He climbed in behind the wheel and started the engine. Through the rolled down window, he leaned his head out and connected to Ethan again. "If you ever want to talk … when, if, you're ever ready to listen to why I left… Well, you know where to find me."

"Why did you come back here anyway?" The question, the *need* to know, escaped Ethan before he could hide it. "Why, after all this time?"

"Oh, I thought you would have figured that out by now." From across the twenty feet that separated them, Ethan felt stripped bare with one thorough look from his teenage crush. Aidan added, "I came back for you."

Before Ethan could utter a word, Aidan slid the glasses on and drove away.

———

AIDAN WATCHED QUIETLY AS THE two other people who owned his heart studied his new place. The small house wasn't much. It was provided to him as part of his job as fire chief, so it wasn't like he'd chosen it, but still, he wanted his brother and sister to like it.

Maddie and Devlin. Fuck, it felt good to look at them and know they wouldn't be gone from his life in another two weeks, not to be seen again for another six months. He was home and he wanted more than just about anything to feel like he was part of a family again. Christ, he wanted Ethan to be his family too, but right now, he started with blood, with his siblings.

"So," Aidan broke the silence as he ended the tour in the small, antiquated kitchen, "this is where I'll be living. I've got steaks and potatoes with all kinds of stuff for toppings, and the makings for a fully-loaded salad, and I have beer -- but not for you." He pointed at his sister, who was only seventeen. "About the beer, I mean, not the food. You can eat. Oh," he waved his arm toward the table, "and I bought a chocolate cake for dessert." The dark, rich-looking confection sat right in the middle, under a plastic dome protector. He lifted the package of steaks off the oven and held it in the air. "These looked like the best the grocery store had to offer, and I have a grill out back. Who wants to eat?"

The two people in front of him burst out laughing. They both had dark hair, like his. Maddie's was long and wavy down her back, and Devlin's looked trim and neat, like Aidan's. Where Aidan had the green eyes of his mother, his brother and sister both had the pale gray, almost silvery gaze of their father. Right now, both sets of gray eyes twinkled, laughing at him from across the kitchen.

Aidan's hand came down, and the steaks thudded on the counter. "What?"

Maddie arched a brow, and Aidan swore she had the confidence of a woman twice her age. "I think you might have forgotten a lace tablecloth and candlelight as the last touches to drive everything home." She smiled, big and cheeky. "Not trying too hard or anything, bro, huh?"

Devlin covered his mouth, and Aidan knew his brother tried not to laugh again.

Aidan's face heated, and he grinned sheepishly. He leaned against the counter and tension he hadn't even been aware he'd been holding uncoiled and let him breathe a little easier. "That obvious, am I?"

Devlin put about an inch of space between his thumb and pointer finger. "Might be coming on just a bit strong." His voice held humor, not judgment. "Just a hair."

"Sorry, guys." Aidan felt all kinds of foolish that he'd been so damn obvious. "I just... It's just... Look, I know I wasn't around much when you were growing up." He looked to his sister. "Especially you, Maddie. I just want you to know that I'm serious here. I'm home to stay, and I want to try and be as good a sibling to each of you as you are to each other." Their mother had passed away two years ago, and their father no longer lived in Redemption. Rather than Maddie moving back to Texas with their dad, Devlin had taken her in, and for all intents and purposes had become her legal guardian.

Maddie turned to Devlin, and cocked her head to the side. "Do you think we've been standoffish with our big brother since he's come home? Do you think he doesn't know we want him with us?"

"Don't know." Devlin's gaze narrowed, and he pursed his lips. "Maybe he needs a little demonstration, just so he's not so insecure anymore."

"Yeah, because that's just sad," Maddie went on. "We can't have our fire chief looking so pathetic." Maddie and Devlin traded a truly conspiratorial look that only the closest siblings can pull off ... and then rushed Aidan with fingers outstretched.

Aidan reached out his arms. "Wait!" Too late, his brother and sister overtook him and attacked his sides and belly with pokes and tickles, and rained kisses all over his face.

Choking with laughter, and trying to squirm out of the tickling, Aidan took the ribbing with good humor and let it sink right into his heart. He'd lost a lot of time with these two, and it squeezed his chest that they could still be so open and accept him back into their lives.

When he couldn't take any more of the tickling, he finally said, "All right, all right, all right; I believe we're okay." With tears streaming down his face, Aidan maneuvered out of Dev and Maddie's hold. Chuckling, he realized his cheeks ached from laughing and smiling. Turning, he faced the other two, and sobered. "It was the chocolate cake that did it." He put a most serious expression on his face as he pulled the lid off the dessert. "Wasn't it."

"You got it," Maddie said.

"It does look good," Devlin observed, as he leaned in and eyed the cake.

Aidan dug a hand into the gooey goodness. "Then we shouldn't let it go to waste." He flung first, hitting Devlin square in the chest, starting a food fight that Aidan later welcomed having to clean up the mess.

Jesus, it was good to be home.

———

LAUGHING, AIDAN LED THE WAY into the station and moved to Engine 1. Running his fingers along the immaculately kept vehicle, he turned to the small crowd of firefighters and worked his way through the line of three men and one woman until he hit on the one he wanted. "Details, people. The devil lives in the details. And today I see some smudges on the paintjob. I think this baby needs work top to bottom. As the probie," he focused on Dev, "it looks like that job falls to you."

"What the fuck?" Devlin groaned. Good-natured ribbing and some "get to its" went up from the small crowd.

"Actually…" Ethan's voice, already familiar again with just that one meeting, broke into the crowd noise, drawing Aidan's full attention. Ethan entered the firehouse through the open garage door, the early evening sunlight behind him throwing him into shadows. Moving to the crowd, Ethan came into focus, and Aidan swallowed hard at the picture the man made in a white button-down shirt and jeans. Ethan's attention moved across Dev and the others, but then came to rest solely on Aidan. "Dev has been here for six months. You only officially started today. I think that technically makes you the probie, boss." Ethan raised a brow. "That sound about right?"

"Ooh," "Hell, yeah," and "Burn," rang out in the small group, followed by even more hooting. Aidan's people were clearly all comfortable around each other, and used to a causal atmosphere with the boss. As long as they did their jobs and managed the workload without any whining, Aidan had no problem with that arrangement. In fact, he preferred it.

Aidan shared a discreet glare with Ethan, one that had a history of being able to read each other's moods and thoughts. They picked the signals right back up, as if they'd never spent thirteen years apart. *You'll pay for that*, was sent from Aidan to Ethan. *Just try something, you bastard*, came back to Aidan, with another raised brow. Aidan smiled. He could work with anger. Indifference would have killed him.

Even if he did deserve it.

"Okay," Aidan stayed on Ethan for just one minute, "while I would argue that probie technically refers to the person who is newest to fighting fires and on probation, I will concede a good argument," he turned to his brother, "and help you detail Engine 1. But make no mistake, you will help."

"Fine." Dev threw up his hands. "Whatever works for you, boss. It's not like I've never done it before…"

At that point, the rest of Devlin's sentence became a buzz of white noise in Aidan's ears. Aidan watched Ethan cross the garage and lean into Kara -- Aidan's only female on the crew -- and press a kiss high on her cheek. The tall redhead smiled and did the same to Ethan, and any fool could see their complete comfort with each other. In fact, none of his other men much acknowledged the exchange, all the proof needed to show that they had witnessed these little intimacies before.

What the fuck?

"You ready to go?" Ethan slipped his hand in Kara's.

"I'm good. My purse is in the car," Kara answered. "I want to run by the house and shower before we go. I stink." She laughed, and so did everyone else.

Aidan had put Devlin and this first group of volunteers through the physical paces today in an effort to gauge the stamina side of their physical strength. He didn't care that they didn't get paid more than a stipend for doing this good work, they still needed to be able to handle the force in the hoses or carry a person out of a building when that terrible day actually came.

"Can we run by my house?" Kara asked Ethan. "I'll be fast as lightning. I promise we won't be late."

"No problem," Ethan agreed. "But we should get going."

Ethan tugged Kara to the open door. She waved, calling back to a stocky black guy, a fifteen-year volunteer veteran,

"Thanks for covering for me, Pete. I owe you."

Pete winked. "I'll find a way to get that payment, doll. Don't you worry."

As soon as Ethan and Kara were out of sight, Pete turned to another man, Coop, a guy with only two years volunteer service under his belt. "I sure hope she's okay." Pete blinked, and Aidan could have sworn the man's eyes started to brim with wetness. "Sure hate to see the woman suffering all over again."

Aidan's head spun in a fast circle. "What?" He grabbed Pete before he joined the others, all likely heading for the showers. "Wait a second, Pete." How in the hell did a medical issue about one of his volunteers not get even a Cliffs Notes sentence in Roger's sporadic records? "Is there something wrong with Kara that I need to know about?"

"Not Kara," Pete said, a hint of a wobble in his voice. "Ethan's mom. Poor woman beat cancer once. Why in the hell did it have to come back?"

Aidan stumbled. What? Ethan's mother had cancer?

Apparently not for the first time.

Shit.

CHAPTER THREE

Aidan banged on the cabin door, cursing himself for violating Ethan's request to keep their new relationship strictly business. Aidan argued that extenuating circumstances were involved. He'd stayed away for twenty-four hours; he couldn't take any more than that. The man's mother was sick, for Christ's sake. That changed everything.

"Open the damn door, Ethan!" Aidan banged again, uncaring about how loud he got. Ethan didn't have any neighbors close by, and Aidan knew Kara wasn't here. In an effort to point out the nights when she absolutely could not take an overnight shift at the firehouse, the woman had been quick to sit down with Aidan to go over her shift schedule at the hospital where she worked as an ER nurse.

Thursday was one of those nights.

"You always were a stubborn jackass," Aidan muttered into the darkness. Frustration, worry, and years of his own neglect in regard to this man hit him hard in the gut. "I can stand here all night if that's what it takes." His voice softened, and he caressed the smooth wood of the door, wishing it were Ethan. "I just want to talk to you for a few minutes. That's all I ask."

Dejected after another long silence, he took a step away from the door. Then it hit Aidan that Ethan's dog wasn't barking up a storm. He redoubled his efforts, this time adding the doorbell to the mix. "Ethan! Are you okay? Why isn't your dog barking? Damn you, I'm about two seconds away from breaking this door down and you fucking know I can do it!"

Within seconds, lights blazed from inside the cabin, setting the porch in a soft glow through the tall windows on either side of the door. Aidan backed off his hammering just as Ethan yanked open the door.

Bare-chested and his blond hair mussed, Ethan looked sexier than Aidan had ever seen him. He wore navy blue sweats and nothing else. "Oz is not here," Ethan informed him. "Otherwise, he'd be doing more than barking; he'd damn well have your ass chewed off by now for harassing his master." Ethan scratched his flat, ripped stomach, and Aidan's mouth went drier than an Arizona summer. "Now, what the hell do you want? You woke me up."

Aidan snapped his focus back up and narrowed his gaze on Ethan. "Liar. You never could fall asleep before midnight." He pushed up the cuff of his long sleeve shirt and glanced at his watch. "It's barely eleven."

"You don't know me anymore, Morgan." Everything seemed to pull straight and tight along the length of Ethan's body. The protective motion tore Aidan apart. "A lot has changed since you left."

All of the righteous air went right out of Aidan. "I know." He pushed through the tightness closing his throat and said, "And I swear I want to explain myself and try to make it up to you, when you're ready to listen."

"I don't care." Ethan's lips thinned to a pursed line. "Not anymore."

Fuck. Aidan moved closer anyway. "I heard about your mom. Why didn't you tell me she was sick?"

Ethan just stood there and somehow achieved the impossible. He grew stiffer and even more still.

"Ethan."

A hint of life suddenly sparked in Ethan's eyes, flaring the blue for just a split second. "Oh, and when should I have shared my troubles with you, Aidan?" he said, his voice edged with ice. "During one of the many times you invited me out to visit you, or when you came home? Or maybe during one of the lengthy phone calls, or letters, or emails we shared where we made sure to keep up to date with each other lives. Which one of those scenarios should I have taken the time to tell you that my mom was ravaged by cervical cancer a year after you left, so fucking bad that my big, strong dad left us, leaving me and Wyn to take care of her and fend for ourselves, with only his guilt money to get us through it. Should I have tracked you down to tell you how goddamned elated we were when she fought her way through it to remission, only to have it attack her again last year? You tell me, Aidan. When should I have shared all this information with my *best*," he threw his hands up and made air quotes with his fingers, "*friend?*"

Aidan rubbed his face, and swore to God he could already feel new lines etched into his flesh. "Look," he tried again, "can I at least come inside so we can talk? While we stand here shouting at each other, we're also issuing an open invitation to every bug in the neighborhood to take up residence in your home. I don't think you want an infestation just so you can stand your ground."

"Sure. Why the hell not?" Ethan threw the door open wide. "Come on in." He made a sweeping gesture with his arm, but it could not have been less welcoming. "Say what's on your mind so that you can get right the hell back out."

Aidan stepped over the threshold One glance took in the cabin, and he instantly traveled back in time. He whistled, low and long, as he put his head on a swivel. "It's just like you always wanted." His voice went hushed, almost in reverence of the open space. The entire floor was one big, open room, with a kitchen to the right, and an area to sit and relax to the left. Toward the back of the cabin sat a big bed and dresser, and another pair of comfortable chairs with a small table in between them. An opening in the wall on the left would lead to a bathroom and a mud/washroom; Aidan didn't have to peek down it to know. Ethan had talked about this cabin often during their friendship.

But the focal point of the entire place, the most important part of Ethan's childhood vision, left Aidan breathless. The back wall was no wall at all, but instead a full picture window, with just a low runner of cushions along a long window seat that went from one wall to the other. Holy mother, it was like living outside, with all of the comforts of indoors.

Everything Ethan had ever wanted in the cabin of his dreams. One that when hearing about it made Aidan ache to live in it too.

Ethan brushed past Aidan and threw himself on a mocha-colored suede couch.

With his mouth still agape, Aidan followed the man into the living area. "Holy shit, Ash. I can't believe you built our house."

"I didn't build *our* house." Ethan shot right back up and stalked Aidan, getting right in his face. "I built *my* cabin, with a friend. I wanted this long before I ever met you, and there wasn't any way I was letting the fact that I let you share it for five minutes kill my dream. You don't have a damn thing to do with this place, so don't go getting any ideas about moving in."

"Oh?" Aidan's blood quickly came to a boil, and his breathing grew more erratic with every second Ethan invaded his personal space. Christ, all the musky male smells went right to Aidan's head. Standing in the home of their teenage dreams didn't do a damn thing to put a damper on his ever-present need for this man. Years and years of going without the only person he had ever wanted spilled over, with no way for Aidan to stop the flood. "I might not have ever lived here with you, but it's a damn sight more my place than it'll ever be Kara's, I'll tell you that right now. I don't have to have shared this space with you to know that you've never laid your body down on that bed," he reached back and pointed with his arm without ever looking away from Ethan, "and had wet dreams about fucking *her*. You don't want her sexually, and whatever the hell you and I ever are or aren't to each other in the future doesn't change that. You don't dream about fucking pussy, Ash. You dream about sinking your cock into a tight, male ass, and it's wrong to let Kara think anything different."

"You don't know anything about me anymore, Aidan, and you certainly don't know anything about me and Kara, so don't assume that you do. You haven't been around to know what I desire anymore, one way or the other." Ethan poked at Aidan's chest with each word he spoke, pushing Aidan in a backward walk with each spearing touch. "And I already fucking told you," the back of Aidan's thighs hit the kitchen table, bowing him backward, "*don't*," he growled the word, "call me Ash."

Aidan burned with life under his skin, and his entire body hummed in a way it hadn't done in thirteen years. Ethan rode his front with less than half a dozen inches between them, and pure passion, even if it was mixed with something more volatile, charged the air around them. Their chests heaved and sharp puffs of warm breath came out of each man in tango, mingling in the air. Ethan had his fists planted on either side of Aidan's hips, and a decidedly hard ridge grazed the inside of Aidan's thigh. *Goddamn, he feels so fucking right against me.* Aidan had never wanted anything more in his life.

Aidan's focus drifted to Ethan's lips, and he studied the fullness of the lower one. His cock twitched as he thought about the many places he had put that mouth in all of his fantasies, and when he brought his gaze back up to Ethan's, he knew they all showed in his stare.

He licked the edge of his lip and imagined it was Ethan's. "When you get into a shouting match with Kara," he looked down to Ethan's crotch, and then came back up, "does she make you hard, like you are now?"

"I'm not --"

"Yes," Aidan leaned in, their lips so unbearably close he trembled with it, "you are."

Ethan opened his mouth, and Aidan stole whatever he wanted to say with a searing kiss. Their lips fused in a frantic maelstrom, and it was as if time slipped away. Ethan melted, groaning as he clutched Aidan's face in a tight grip, bruisingly so, and pushed his way inside for a deeper plundering. For Aidan, the sting of pain had never been sweeter. He opened up to let Ethan take as much of his mouth as he could, uncaring that it was untried and messy, just that it was Ethan, and nothing else mattered.

Aidan wrapped his arms around Ethan and tugged the

man between his legs, getting every inch of hard body he could rubbing against his. Ethan moaned and jerked. At the same time, he reached down, grabbed Aidan's hips, and thrust his cock against the bulge in Aidan's jeans.

Aidan went up in flames. Never, ever had it been like this for him. Never in their time apart had he had what he wanted. Ethan.

All of Ethan.

Aidan broke the kiss, panting heavily as he stared into the blur of Ethan's blue eyes. "More." His voice sounded gritty to his own ears, but he couldn't pull himself together and regain some distance. "I need to know more." He scraped his fingertips down Ethan's sinewy, mouth-watering back. When he got to the elastic waist of Ethan's snug sweats, Aidan kept right on going, reaching the heaven of Ethan's smooth, tight ass. "Oh, Christ…" Aidan kneaded the firm flesh in his hands, and began to kiss his way down Ethan's throat to his stunning chest. Heat from Ethan scorched Aidan's lips and tongue, but he couldn't stop licking a trail over the man's pecs. "You taste so damn good, man."

"You shouldn't…" Ethan started. Right then, though, Aidan latched onto a copper colored disc and flicked his tongue over the tip, teasing the tiny nubbin to a hard point. In response, Ethan buried his hands in Aidan's hair and dug his fingers in, pulling until it hurt. "Ahh, fuck, fuck…" Ethan paused, groaning when Aidan bit, and then soothed with a lick. "Shouldn't…"

Unable to stop, Aidan kissed his way across the smooth surface of Ethan's chest, inhaling sweat of the day and the pungent green scents of the outdoors, something that had always been attached to Ethan. He nuzzled in on the other side and ministered lavish attention on that flat circle of darker skin too.

Ethan's fingers scraped across Aidan's scalp, and he uttered, "Shouldn't do this." Even as he said it, he held Aidan to him, rather than shoving him away.

"Wanted you forever, Ash," Aidan confessed, his voice raw with emotion. "Ached for you." He pressed a kiss against steaming skin, loving the hot feel of it against his sensitized lips. Ethan's hands stayed in his hair, but Aidan couldn't slow down. He dipped his head and started to kiss his way down Ethan's torso. Dropping to his knees, he buried his face against Ethan's stomach, spilling everything going on inside him as he pushed Ethan's sweats down to his hips, springing his erection free, where the tip grazed Aidan's neck and left a smear of early cum. "Never stopped needing you." Christ, the smells of pre-ejaculate and man assaulted Aidan's nostrils, dizzying him in its intensity. Swirling a lick into Ethan's belly button, Aidan inhaled again, and continued his journey downward. He wanted to learn every inch of this man intimately and visit places he had never gone during that afternoon they'd shared in the woods.

Like his cock, with something more than a shared handjob.

Kneeling down before Ethan, in this cabin, with Ethan's

penis rearing hard and heavy only inches from Aidan's face...
Damn. Never in Aidan's life had he ever felt more like he'd
found the place he was meant to be. "Christ, the years only
made you more beautiful." Afraid he'd given Ethan too much
emotion too fast, Aidan opened up and took Ethan inside,
sucking his best friend's length halfway to his throat in one
hard drag.

A strangled noise rumbled through Ethan. He immediately
doubled over and braced his hands against the table. "Oh ...
oh, Aidan. God, that's so good." He pumped his hips, filling
Aidan's mouth the rest of the way with salty, firm cock, forcing
Aidan to pull off before he choked. He had never done this
before, and he didn't want to embarrass himself. He quickly
wrapped his hand around the lower half of Ethan's prick and
started to jerk him off, trying to keep a rhythm between his
hand, his sucking, and Ethan's fucking of his mouth. *Oh shit,
I like the visual of that.* He wanted Ethan crazy for him all the
time, and fucking him in every way.

Aidan redoubled his efforts and swirled his tongue all
around Ethan's dick, lapping over every inch of exposed skin,
and teased over the slit too. Ethan bucked his hips when
Aidan did that, giving Aidan a tell-tale movement of pleasure
he couldn't deny. Aidan looked up as best he could from his
position and found Ethan's head turned down, the edge of his
lip sucked between his teeth, and his eyes open, rapt, on what
Aidan did to him. Their gazes connected in the shadow their
bodies created, and Aidan never looked away as he went down

on Ethan's length, stuffing as much hard cock in his mouth as he could take, filling himself with *Ethan*.

Not even close to enough, he reached between Ethan's spread legs and rolled the heavy weight of his balls, forcing a moan and a sharp exhale of breath from the other man. Ethan looked almost tormented, and Aidan's own cock pushed hard against his jeans, needful of release. Thinking about how he might be able to come tonight himself, Aidan slipped his hand behind Ethan's testicles and pressed the heel against the thin membrane of flesh. Ethan jumped, and Aidan pushed this thing a little further. Slipping his fingers up Ethan's crease, he came across the textured skin he had wanted to know forever. He pressed against Ethan's tight little asshole, and at the same time dragged with powerful suction up the length of his pulsing, hot cock.

"Ohhhh fuck." Ethan's lips pulled back, baring his teeth as his body locked tight. "Aidan, Aidan…" As that name slipped from his lips, his eyes darkened with rich blue and burned bright. Staring down at Aidan, his voice almost without sound, Ethan keened, "Close … so close." Aidan opened up wide and took Ethan to his throat, pushing the man even closer to the edge. He teased the line of veins on the underside with the flat of his tongue, moaning at the richness of male taking over his mouth. Christ, Aidan wanted everything with Ethan, starting with drinking him down as he came. He licked again, and sucked, letting his throat massage Ethan's tip. Then he rubbed the tip of his finger against Ethan's pucker again.

Ethan didn't stand a chance. "Ohh God, it's happening…"
He pulled his hips back and thrust hard. His lips parted,
throwing his face into a thing of beauty as orgasm took over his
being. His penis swelled within the confines of Aidan's mouth.
A second later he spurted, and bitter pulses of hot cum spilled
free, coating Aidan's tongue, and cheeks, and then his throat,
giving him a piece of Ethan he'd never had before. Aidan drank
from Ethan's cock greedily, swallowing down every last drop of
his man's seed.

Fuck, he wanted to bend Ethan over and screw him with a
need that felt akin to breathing, but Aidan knew he wouldn't
last long enough to even get his dick inside Ethan's ass, let alone
achieve one stroke in that tight, hot channel.

Aidan shot up to standing. In one motion, he grabbed
Ethan's hand and shoved it down his pants, wincing as their
hands yanked on his pubic hair before he got them wrapped
around his straining erection. "Touch me, Ash." He held his
palm over the back of Ethan's hand, whimpering with need.
His balls pulled up tight enough to border on pain with the
need to come, something Aidan somehow knew he couldn't
make happen on his own. Still, Ethan's hand lay flat against
Aidan's dick, but didn't move. Aidan looked into Ethan's eyes,
and hid nothing in his own. "Please, Ethan. Hold it. Make me
come."

A battle raged in the man in front of him, hardening his
handsome face. Biting off a curse, Ethan swooped in and
ravaged Aidan with a brutal kiss. Teeth clinked and angry bites

left small cuts on lips, but Ethan took hold of Aidan's rigid prick and jerked him off with one good, hard pull.

Aidan cried out, he didn't know if in pain or joy, or a combination of both. Nothing inside him cared. He dug his fingers into Ethan's hold of him, shuddering and reveling in this man touching him and kissing him again. Ethan milked Aidan's length and slid the pad of his callused finger across the tip and sensitive underside, curling Aidan's toes.

Orgasm raced through Aidan's spine and belly to his cock, and he started to come. "Don't pull away." He pushed Ethan's hand down to cover his slit and accept his seed, needing desperately to make Ethan feel what barely one stroke of his hand did to Aidan's body. Aidan thrust his tongue into Ethan's mouth and kissed him with every minute of missing him while they had been apart. At the same time, his penis pulsed with his release, over and over again, and he spit hot jets of thick cum into Ethan's waiting hand.

Both men heaved with gulping breaths in the aftermath. Their violent kiss eventually slowed, and they broke apart with the end of Aidan's orgasm. Foreheads fell to rest against each other, and gazes met, blurred in such close proximity. Aidan smiled, unable to stop the motion from wrapping itself around his lips. Ethan smiled back, the grin lopsided and familiar. It snaked right into Aidan's heart and wrapped him up tight, just as it had so long ago.

As quickly as Ethan smiled, his stare changed to something full of dark clouds. Instantly, he tore his hand out of Aidan's pants, as if burned. He yanked his sweats up and took two very deliberate steps backward, putting the stiffness Aidan had quickly become accustomed to seeing back in place.

"All right," Ethan said, "so you proved I still want you." He lifted his hands, but when his focus strayed to the sheen of Aidan's cum covering the left one, he quickly put them down to his sides. He walked sideways toward the front of the cabin, as if afraid to take his eyes off Aidan for one second. "Doesn't change anything. It doesn't mean I want you in my life, and it doesn't mean I trust you for one goddamned second. I don't. We are nothing more to each other now than we were when you walked inside my house fifteen minutes ago." He threw the door open, and held it wide. "You need to leave."

"Ash."

"Go." Ethan clutched the door so hard Aidan thought he might break a chunk off with his bare hand. "Right. Now."

Aidan slumped against the table, but then picked himself up and made his way to the door. *Smooth move, Morgan. Going down on him before you've barely said hello. Now he really thinks your reasons for coming here were sincere.*

Aidan paused before stepping outside, but made sure to keep some distance between him and Ethan. He forced himself to face Ethan even though he knew heat flamed inside, and his face and neck burned red. "I really did come here to ask about your mom, and to see how you were doing."

"I'm fine." Ethan's voice was clipped. "My mom is fine, and my brother is fine too." His jaw clicked though, and his hand trembled slightly on the doorknob. "Now you have the official update, so you can leave."

"If you need anything at all from me…" Christ, Aidan couldn't stand leaving things between them so unresolved. "If you can't take your shift at the station…"

Ethan snorted. "A little over a week ago you refused to let me quit."

Aidan stuffed down the need to shake this man until he let go of just a little bit of this stubborn stoicism. "This is different."

"I don't need your pity."

"Damn it, I didn't mean it like that."

"The one way to guarantee you stop saying the wrong thing is to just get the hell out."

"Fine." Aidan would get nowhere tonight, he could see it in the familiar set to Ethan's jaw. "But I'm here, whenever you're ready to talk, or listen."

"I already have people for that. Thank you."

People who hadn't run and left him alone, Aidan heard the unspoken words under the hard tone. "Okay, then. I won't push anymore. Whatever you want." Commanding his legs to move, Aidan walked out onto the porch. "Goodnight. I'll see you at the station for drills on Monday."

"I'll be there."

Ethan slammed the door before Aidan could say another word.

Holding his breath, Ethan waited for Aidan's truck to start, and then slid down the door to the floor. *Good God, what have I done?* His heart raced so fast he swore he would be able to see it if he looked in a mirror. He put his hand against his chest, as if that could help slow it down, and in the process smeared Aidan's seed against his skin. Unable to take his fingers away, Ethan spread the sticky substance across his chest, *over his heart*, aching with how damn good it felt to be with Aidan again. It wasn't so much the blowjob, although, fuck, that had been insane. Rather, for a few minutes there, it felt like the years apart had slipped away and they were the two eighteen-year-old kids who'd planned to bum around the States for a few years before coming back to Redemption to build a life together.

How the comfort of that memory had lulled Ethan, allowing it to pull him under the tide of passion, something he had only ever felt for Aidan.

He ran away and left you without a word. He never attempted to get in touch with you to see how you were, not even once. Ethan's chest constricted, his heart aching over how damn badly he'd needed Aidan during that first bout of his mother's cancer, and the man had been nowhere to lean on. Now Aidan wanted to step in and be Ethan's savior, hold him in his arms while he grieved about the pain his mother suffered, something Ethan couldn't do a damn thing to stop.

The ring of his phone jerked Ethan out of his self-pity. He sprang upright and raced to it, snatching it up before a third ring sounded. "Hello?" He stopped to swallow in an effort to erase the breathlessness in his voice. He knew it could only be one person. "What's wrong, man?"

His brother Wyn's familiar gruff tone came through the line. "She's not feeling too good tonight, E. Oz doesn't seem to be helping her settle down. Maybe you should come sit with us for a while."

Damn. His dog usually did his mother a lot of good. "Sit tight." Ethan moved to his dresser in two strides. "I'll be there soon."

He clicked end, and Aidan's words, *I'm here if you need me,* whispered in his ear, as if the man stood right at his side. Ethan looked at the phone, moving his focus over each number that would get him Aidan.

Shaking his head, Ethan tossed the phone on the bed, the first button never touched.

CHAPTER FOUR

Steeling himself for anything, Ethan unlocked the front door to his old home and let himself inside the stylishly decorated house. Shaking his head, as he always did, he whispered, "Good on you, Mom," and then unzipped and laid his hooded sweatshirt on a silk covered chair.

When his mother's cancer had returned thirteen months ago, and she knew she would be weak and home much of the time, she had taken a good chunk of the blood money their father had left them and had the house redecorated from top to bottom. Ethan and Wyn had already made it clear they did not want their father's money, and would not accept it if she saved it and willed it to them after she passed. So on the day she'd discovered the cancer had returned, and they all sat silently in the living room trying to digest the news, she'd up and said, "Screw it. If these are the walls I have to look at when I die, they'd damn well better be beautiful."

Feeling the familiar tightness constrict his throat, Ethan took a moment in the foyer to pull himself together.

As he counted to ten and let out a slow breath, Wyn came out of the kitchen, a can of Pepsi in his hand. "Hey." He kept his voice hushed, and leaned his shoulder against the archway. "She and Oz are in the living room watching TV. Some sort of ultimate fighting cage match or something. I swear to God our mother has a violent streak that she has kept hidden for most of our lives. The things I've learned spending this extra time here would make our priest blush." They shared a chuckle, but it sounded forced and they both knew it.

As much as she hated it, ten weeks ago Jayne Ashworth had started requiring someone be in her home with her at all times. A lot of time spent arguing on the phone had gotten a nurse on the premises during the day, but after the nursing shift ended, it became a task taken up by her sons, their aunt, and a few friends. Ethan and Wyn alternated weeks where they would each take two nights, then one, and then back to two sleeping in their childhood home. They were blessed their mother had friends who loved her dearly, and between their Aunt Estelle and those women, Jayne was never without help when needed.

Not that she ever liked asking for it.

Like mother like sons.

Ethan looked at his younger brother and knew the tired

and worried expression on Wyn's face matched his when he looked in a mirror. Wyn was a good cop and an even better man, but fuck, there were those moments when watching a loved one grow more ill every day beat the life out of the best of people.

"What made you call me tonight?" Ethan asked. "Is she feeling sick or throwing up? Is she refusing to eat?" Within the last week, their mother's appetite had dropped drastically.

"No, she did pretty good tonight, and the nurse said she ate some lunch today too. It's not that." Wyn fiddled with the pop-top on his can of soda, and shifted his weight from one foot to the other. "Listen, you know what, I probably shouldn't even have called you. It's just more of a feeling, something when I looked into her eyes that panicked me. I'm sorry I pulled you out of bed. I know you're exhausted."

"No more than you." Ethan looked into the brown eyes of his brother, and a hint of unsteadiness there made his decision for him. "I'm not going anywhere."

"Thanks." Wyn ran his hand through his dark hair, and then left his palm there as if he required the assistance to hold his head upright. "Maybe it's me who needs you more than her; I don't know."

A feminine rumble sounded through the hallway walls. "You could both go out for a beer and take a break!" Their mother's voice cut through the air, surprising in its strength. "I'll live for an hour without one of you holding my hand." Ethan and Wyn glanced at the entrance to the living room and then back at each other, their faces pulling with humor. "I have cancer, you know," she finished smartly. "I'm not deaf. I can hear every darn word you say."

Shaking their heads, Ethan and Wyn moved into the living room, smiling sheepishly.

Ethan walked to the couch, dipped down, and pecked a kiss to his mother's head. Her tresses still held a rich mahogany color, with only a touch of gray. Oz lay spread out on the couch next to her with his giant head on her lap.

"Hi, Mom." Ethan gave his dog a good scratch behind the ears before sitting down on the other end of the couch. "So, what's this I hear about you watching ultimate fighting matches?" He raised a brow her way. "You never watch that when I'm here."

"You're never here on the right night, kiddo." Jayne Ashworth might have lost some of her physical abilities, as well as look frail as a newborn bird, but her mind still worked quicker than just about anyone Ethan knew. She grabbed his focus and stayed right with him. "So what's this I hear about Aidan Morgan being back in town?"

Ethan flashed back to Aidan's mouth wrapped around his cock, along with the incredible feel of it and brief minutes of perfect connection, before Ethan had remembered the past and put a stop to where things might have gone next. Just thinking about lying face down on a bed and letting Aidan split him open and claim his ass for the first time rushed a quick shiver through Ethan. *No.* God, he could not deal with Aidan and the feelings the man stirred in him -- not right now.

Stiffening his resolve, Ethan said, "I'd rather talk about the ultimate fighting."

"Of course you would, dear," Jayne replied. "And just for tonight, I'll let you get away with it." He looked into his mother's rheumy blue eyes and swore to God she knew all of the secrets he had never shared.

Without missing a beat, she turned to her other son where he sat in a wingback chair. "As for you, Wyn Joseph Ashworth," she held out her hand in Wyn's direction, "give me that soda. You don't need the sugar." Wyn handed it over, and laughter sparked in Jayne's eyes. "But I do." She took a big gulp and then let out a very unladylike burp.

This time, the laughter bursting from both brothers was real.

———

"COME ON, COME ON, COME ON!" Aidan held the stopwatch in his hand, keeping one eye on the seconds ticking away and the other on his crew -- paid and volunteer -- as they donned their turnout gear and SCBA masks. The requirement was from civvies to turnout in one minute or less, and it was necessary training Aidan had to run his firefighters through on a regular basis, no matter how small a task it seemed. To mix it up and give drills like these a bit more variety, Aidan liked to assign each person a position on one of the engines to see if he or she could get to in under the time constraints too.

Four, three, two, one. "Time!" Aidan raised his hands in the air. "Stop where you are."

Everyone froze, and Aidan moved around each engine in a wide circle, assessing where each member had ended, and if all of them had their regulation gear on correctly. Aidan fully expected his full-time guys to be turned out and in place, and in fact would have been damn pissed if they weren't. As he had been learning over the last two weeks since taking charge, his men didn't disappoint. What warmed his heart, and settled some of the nerves he'd experienced since agreeing to take a job in a firehouse that mixed paid and unpaid crew, was that his volunteer staff were almost all in place too. Even the two guys who stood stock-still in mid-run had their helmet and gear on properly; they just hadn't quite made it to the assigned vehicle. Aidan could live with that. They would do a drill like this on a regular basis, and those two men would soon make it to the truck as well.

"All right, guys," Aidan put his hands together in a short, hard clap, "great job, great job. Give yourselves a hand." Everyone jumped off the trucks, hooting and sharing high fives. Aidan nodded at that visual too. Just what he wanted to see. He gave a quick, sharp whistle and drew everyone's attention back to him. "Now take everything off and get it bagged and stored properly in your vehicles. Good lord willing, you'll never need to use it. One final thing." He glanced at his watch. "We have pizza coming as a reward for showing up. It should be here in five minutes."

A whoop of approval went up in the small crowd, making Aidan laugh. Everyone moved quickly and, like he had been doing from the moment tonight's drill had begun, Aidan found himself searching for Ethan, hungry for any piece of the man he could get. Finding him with Kara, their heads together in a quiet conversation, Aidan fought the heat of jealousy, knowing that by staying away from Redemption for so long he had no right to wish he were the one Ethan confided in. Didn't stop Aidan from feeling that stab of pain though. He turned away, cursing under his breath.

Fucking pull yourself together, man. This is your job. Behave like a professional. More than that, respect Ethan's request and leave him the hell alone.

Aidan dug his fingers into his palms, psyched himself up to be a man, and turned back to the group. Scanning the area, his gaze settled on a clipboard hanging on the wall. "Don't forget to sign the call-in sheet, guys, or you won't get the timed credit for showing up." His focus darted to Kara. "And, gal," he added. "I apologize."

"Not necessary, Chief." Kara smiled, and goddamnit if Aidan understood exactly why Ethan desired her company. She fucking lit up the room. "I hope when I'm here, I am just one of the guys. Just like any other woman who might one day decide to step up to the job."

"I'm working on it," Aidan said. "Believe me, Kara, I'd like at least another ten volunteers, so at the very least you guys don't have to do an overnight every single week. I don't much care if they're men or women, as long as they can pass the training and are willing to put in the commitment."

A distinctly familiar *ahem* sounded from behind. Aidan turned and found his sister standing in the center of the open garage door, her hands on her waist. "Then why won't you let me join the crew?"

Aidan rolled his eyes. Christ, she would bring this up in front of his people. "Not until you're eighteen, Maddie, and that's final."

Maddie's hands went to her hips. "I'll have you know I read the rules, and as long as I have parental or a legal guardian's consent, I can join right now." Her attention flitted off one brother and landed on the other. "That would be you, Dev."

Dev crossed his arms in a stance identical to Aidan's. "Not until you're eighteen, Maddie, and that's final."

Right then, a young man came up behind Maddie and stooped down until his mouth was at her ear. "Sounds like you just got told, M & M."

Maddie whipped around and glared. The man narrowed his stare right back.

M & M? Aidan growled as he wondered what in the hell that was about. Oh, Maddie Morgan. M & M, like the candy. *So fucking clever.* Aidan growled again. He did not like hearing some guy calling Maddie a nickname he had never heard anyone else use before, especially when the man was clearly older than his sister. Aidan didn't like how the dude put his mouth so close to Maddie's ear either. He took a step forward.

Right then Ethan's voice filled the room, touching over Aidan's flesh. "Quit being a jackass, Wyn."

This was little Wyn? Wyn Ashworth, Ethan's little brother, all grown up. Shit. When had he gotten so damn big? *When you went away, asshole.* Guilt answered Aidan's own question.

Ethan and Kara slung their duffels over their shoulders and moved across the garage to where Maddie and Wyn stood.

"I have a feeling Maddie could kick the butt of anyone here, including you," Ethan said, as he shoved his brother playfully in the shoulder. "She'll make a great volunteer firefighter." Ethan leaned down, kissed Maddie's cheek, and then winked. "Next year. Now," he looked over Maddie's head at Wyn, "you come here to make an enemy tonight, or to give me a ride?"

"Everyone is waiting for us." Wyn's tone went stone cold sober. "We should probably go."

Aidan's heart pounded hard as he witnessed how sweetly Ethan treated Maddie, and he wished with every fiber of his being he could just let the man leave without a word. He had a firehouse to maintain though.

"Ethan," he called out, his voice breathy.

Christ, Aidan hoped nobody read anything into his scratchy tone. The dryness in his mouth only got worse when the man in question turned and settled his blue eyes right on Aidan.

"Your shift?" Aidan reminded Ethan. "You're on for the overnight tonight."

"I'll be back," Ethan answered. "Coop said he would cover me for a couple of hours."

"Oh, yeah. Sorry, boss," Coop said from across the room. "Ethan called me yesterday. I mentioned it to AC Pickens and told him I would tell you. Sorry."

Ethan held Aidan's gaze. "So, does that mean we're good?"

"Yeah, sure." Aidan would have to talk to his assistant chief and make sure he noted these changes on the schedule. A lack of good communication between the two men in charge did not look good to the staff. "If you need more time…"

"I don't." Ethan's abrupt tone pierced Aidan in the heart. "I'll be here, just like I said I would."

"All right."

"Hey!" A way too happy delivery boy chose just that moment to join the growing crowd at the open garage door, a stack of pizzas in his arms. "Anybody here order some pizzas?"

The hungry group behind Aidan drowned out his answer, and by the time he finished paying for the pizzas, Ethan, Kara, and Wyn were gone.

———

ETHAN LEANED ON THE BUZZER at the firehouse, exhausted to the bone. He didn't know how much more of teaching full time, coaching the girls' volleyball team, participating in volunteer firefighting, and having his heart torn out seeing his mother's health deteriorate he could take without dropping. *As much as you have to. Just like you did before.*

The door opened, and Coop stood there, his jacket already on and a yawn stretching his jaw. Darkness loomed behind the man, proof that everyone on call tonight had already bedded down for the night.

"Sorry." Guilt ate at Ethan. He wanted to ram his fist into the wall, just to get some release from everything brewing inside him. "Mom got to talking and I didn't want to walk away before she was finished." Emotion strangled Ethan's throat, nearly suffocating him. His mother had gathered her family and friends, deciding not to wait for a will after she was gone from this earth before doling out some sentimental treasures for each of her loved ones. Looking at Coop now, seeing his bloodshot eyes, Ethan felt his normal life slowly unraveling, with no way to put it back together. "I didn't mean to keep you past our agreement. I'll make it up to you. I swear I will."

"Not a problem." Coop gave Ethan's shoulder a squeeze as he moved to the outside, and Ethan moved inside. Coop smiled, and it transformed his fierce looking face. "It's not like I have anyone waiting at home for me, you know?" His almost-black gaze met Ethan's and held. "Any time you need a little extra help, just say the word. We all mean that when we say it, E. Take advantage of us. We want you to. The opportunity will come soon enough where we'll need a favor too. We all know you would step up in a heartbeat and lend a hand."

"Th-thanks." Ethan had a hard time getting words out past the lump in his throat. He made a rough noise before he could continue. "Have a good night. I'll see you next week."

Coop pursed his lips, and nodded. "'Night." Ethan watched until the big man made it to his car and got inside before he stepped back and closed the door. The hushed sounds of the TV Coop must have been watching murmured softly from the shadowed far corner of the room. A flicker of light from the screen flashed softly, hardly cutting across the big, open space.

Dropping his overnight bag to the floor, Ethan took a deep breath in an effort to regulate the unsteadiness in his heartbeat. He knew the guys here at the station just wanted to help, and truthfully, he couldn't have gotten through this last year without them. But each time they showed him a kindness, especially when it was from a big, gruff guy like Coop, it only churned up even more emotion in Ethan -- emotion he already fought like hell to keep pushed down and under control. When Ethan combined that kindness with what he'd had to deal with at his mother's tonight...

"No." Ethan covered his face. His body dropped back against the door as the weight of everything in his daily routine shoved against him, struggling against his strength, fighting to pull him under the current. His voice harsh, he commanded, "No," again, demanding that he pull himself together. If his mother could do it, and *she was the one dying,* for God's sake, Ethan could damn well keep it together too. "No." His voice dropped to a whisper. "No."

Strong arms suddenly encircled him, pulling Ethan against a wide chest, with a scent so masculine and familiar that he shivered.

Aidan. Oh God. It's Aidan.

"Shh, shh," Aidan whispered at his ear. Those incredible

arms rocked Ethan in a tight hold, taking him to a place of safety he hadn't felt in forever. "It's okay, baby." Aidan lulled Ethan with the comfort in his rich voice, and a big hand rubbing a soothing circle into the small of his back. "Just let it go for a few minutes. It's okay. Everyone else is asleep. No one will know but me."

Ethan drifted back in time, to when this man had meant everything to him, to when Ethan had trusted him with the whole of his heart.

God, he needed his best friend again.

In Aidan's arms, Ethan crumbled.

CHAPTER FIVE

Aidan's heart broke for the man trembling in his arms. Everything in him wanted to shield Ethan from all harm and hurts and make sure nothing bad ever touched his life again.

"Tell me." He pressed a kiss to the side of Ethan's head and against his temple. "Tell me what has you so wrecked."

Ethan stiffened immediately and then struggled until he disentangled himself from Aidan's hold. The blue in his eyes shone bright in the shadows, and his jaw kicked up a notch. "I'm fine. I'm here to do a job. I'm not going to fall apart on you, so you don't have to worry."

Fuck the vow to keep my distance. "I'm not worried about your ability to do the job, damn it. I'm worried about you."

Aidan snaked his hand around Ethan's neck and yanked the man in until their foreheads touched. Their gazes clashed, but Aidan didn't let Ethan pull away. "I'm worried you're bottling everything up, just like you used to do when we were younger. I'm worried you're not letting anyone get close enough to you to see the kind of pain you're in, just like you used to do back then too."

Aidan closed his eyes for a just a moment and inhaled that wonderful scent of the outdoors that signaled *Ethan* in his mind. When he opened them back up, he found Ethan's focus right on him. It stirred his cock, and his balls swelled with seed. *Don't kiss him, damn it. Fucking get yourself under control.*

Exhaling through the need for more physical intimacy, Aidan forced himself to suppress it and get them on some neutral ground. "I would also wager you're not eating, so the very least you can do is follow me to the kitchen and finish the pizza I saved for you. At least then I won't worry you're going to pass out should we get a call tonight."

Ethan's stomach rumbled loudly right then, and both men jumped and separated. Ethan's cheeks darkened, and Aidan chuckled.

"I guess I could eat something," Ethan admitted.

Aidan cuffed him on the shoulder. "Yeah, I guess you could. Come on. Follow me and I'll fix you a plate."

Aidan gave the visual of a casual walk, pausing to flip the switch inside the open door, and flooding the big kitchen in fluorescent light. He moved to the fridge, got out the leftover pizza, and flipped open the box as he set it on the counter. He reached into open shelving above, grabbed a thick white plate, and set two oversized slices of pizza on it, one half on top of the other. Going back into the refrigerator, he removed two sodas, popped the top on one and held it out in offering. From the doorway, Ethan paused at the threshold, his attention drifting from the Coke, to the pizza, to Aidan. Aidan waited him out for what felt like an eternity before Ethan finally took the necessary steps into the kitchen to accept the drink.

Ethan glanced down at the pizza. Before taking a slice, he brought his gaze back up to Aidan's. "You remembered." A hint of a smile quirked his lips at the edge.

Pepperoni and mushrooms. *Ethan's favorite.* "Yeah, I did. I even remember that you like it better cold the next day." He nudged the plate in Ethan's direction, and for some fucking reason Aidan could not fathom, his heart raced like mad. When Ethan picked up a slice and took a huge bite, Aidan finally started breathing again. "I remember a lot," he added, unable to help himself. "Even though you must think I left because I didn't care."

Ethan's entire body went rigid. "I don't want to talk about that."

"Then how about what happened tonight?" Aidan pressed. "I can see you're hurting."

His eyes seeming to crystallize like ice, Ethan said, "I'm fine."

"You're not fine, damn it." Aidan slammed his can of soda

down with a hard thunk, splashing liquid onto the counter. "Fuck, why can't you just talk to me, the way you used to do? You could tell me anything, and by virtue of that, you made me want to share things with you. Shit that I never thought I'd share with anybody, I told you, without thinking twice about it."

"Fucking smug asshole!" Ethan dropped his pizza and grabbed Aidan's T-shirt in his fists, shoving him into the counter. His words barely registered in volume, but righteousness infused every fiber of his being, loud enough to blow the roof off the place. "If you could tell me anything, then why didn't you face me like a man all those years ago and tell me why you didn't want me, instead of running away like a pussy!"

Aidan grabbed right back, tangling his hands in Ethan's shirt, struggling against the power of his anger. "Because if I'd seen you, even for one goddamn minute, I would have chosen you, okay! I would have fucking picked you over them, and I would have hated myself and you for doing it!"

"Picked me over who!"

"My brother and sister, damn it!" All of the fight went right out of Aidan, as if he had been holding an enormous bubble inside that finally popped. "Christ, I would have lost my brother and sister if I'd chosen you." His fingers fluttered over Ethan's face, as if he could relearn this person he should have known inside and out by now, but didn't. "I knew if I saw you even one more time to try to explain, the words never would have left my mouth. I would have looked into your beautiful eyes, or heard your voice that makes me so fucking hard, and I would have said 'let's go, let's go right now,' and I would have lost Maddie and Dev forever. I'd already almost lost them once, and I couldn't risk it again." Aidan rubbed his hands up Ethan's chest and then across his shoulders. His heart lurching over that night that had changed his life so long ago, Aidan abruptly pulled away and put some distance between them. He lifted his head, though, and gave Ethan the respect of looking into his eyes. "I'm sorry, but I couldn't do it."

"Do what?" Ethan's head spun with half-information. He backed up until his ass hit the table but managed to get himself into a chair. Kicking out the mismatched one adjacent to him, he looked at it, then looked at Aidan.

Aidan took a step, but quickly stopped. Darting his focus to the chair, he turned back to Ethan without making another move. "You sure? I can go and leave you to eat in peace, if that's what you want."

Ethan exhaled, the sigh reaching every corner of the room. "Don't do this to me, Aidan. Don't mess with my head. Not tonight." He pulled his own chair up to the table and rested his head in his hand. "You've got one chance to explain what you just said to me. You'd better do it quickly, before I change my mind." He watched Aidan where he stood, frozen in place. "Or are you gonna find your legs and run again, instead of giving me the truth?"

"I'm not running from you ever again." The rawness in Aidan's voice caught Ethan in the chest.

Ethan stared as Aidan stood in the too-bright kitchen, his jaw working visibly, drawing attention to the sexy, masculine hardness of his face, different in so many subtle ways from that teenager so long ago. Letting his gaze wander downward, Ethan looked, and his mouth watered at the fit, cut, adult body that was quite different from what he remembered seeing by the creek that magical day. Cursing, Ethan turned his attention to the floor, hating that he still felt such a gut-level attraction to this one man. Only this time it was worse, because he knew Aidan had hurt him, and yet it didn't seem to matter to his thickening cock or needy ass at all. It should fucking *matter* that his guy had broken his heart. His dick should not respond so readily to someone who had caused him such pain.

And yet it did.

Aidan finally walked to the chair and sat down. The proximity only heightened Ethan's awareness, made him want to reach out and feel the stubble covering the lower portion of Aidan's face. Made him ache to get down on his knees and see what it would feel like to have a hard cock in his mouth. No, not *a* hard cock, *Aidan's* hard cock. He pictured Aidan shoving his prick inside, past Ethan's lips, and fucking his face with passionate, vigorous thrusting. His moans would take over the room, echoing against the walls as he buried himself balls deep down Ethan's throat as he shouted and came.

"…everything I'd ever heard her say when she saw stuff

about gay people on TV." Aidan's voice broke into Ethan's lust-filled thoughts and ripped him back into reality. With his forehead furrowing, Aidan sat stock-straight, with only his fingers fiddling with a napkin he'd pulled from a basket sitting in the center of the oversized table. "You dropped me off at home that night and I was so excited about our plans I couldn't keep it off my face. When my mom first asked what was going on, I said it was nothing." Aidan lifted his focus off his hands and met Ethan's gaze. "I wasn't ashamed of you, I just didn't want to get into it with my dad, Dev, and Maddie sitting there watching TV."

His heart thudding hard enough to make him feel sick, Ethan only nodded. God, he couldn't believe he was finally going to get an explanation, and that he was actually sitting here listening to it, after all these years.

"Anyway," Aidan started again, "everyone went to bed eventually, but I couldn't sleep. Christ, Ash, you filled my head, and I couldn't sit or lie still. I just wandered around the house, fiddling with things, all with this stupid smile on my face. One of the times when I wandered into the kitchen, my mom was there. She told me to sit with her for a few minutes, and I did." A small smile lifted the corner of Aidan's mouth, but in a flash, it wobbled, and then it was gone. "She took my hand and told me how proud she was of me because of how I got my life back in order after all the trouble back in Texas."

Ethan knew Aidan had started to hang out with a bad crowd in Texas, getting arrested for vandalism and stealing cars, not listening to his parents, and not respecting their curfew. He'd done some bad shit, but it paled in comparison to most of the rumors that had floated around their high school. The day Aidan had trusted him enough to tell him the truth was one of the best in Ethan's life.

Aidan went on, "I was just sitting there glowing under her praise. On top of her pride in me was my happiness that I knew I had you. I was so fucking psyched that I just blurted out everything. I told her I was in love with you, and that you wanted me too, and that we were gonna be together, and that I'd never been happier or more grateful that she'd moved us all to Redemption. I thought for sure she'd be excited for me. She'd never said anything negative about gay people when we saw something on TV. All I ever heard from her was how terrible it was when she saw things on the news about a gay person getting beat up or killed. But … but…" Aidan paused and ran an unsteady hand through his hair.

Riveted, Ethan covered his mouth, stuffing down the order for Aidan to finish his story. At the same time, he relived that first rush of desire for Aidan from so long ago, where the only thing he had wanted was to offer Aidan comfort when the rich kids in town chose him as their newest target for harassment. Right now, Aidan sat three feet away, wearing that same cloak of quiet strength he'd worn that day outside the fast food joint. Ethan knew that like back then, on the inside, the man's body buzzed with hurt and rage.

Unable to stop himself, Ethan reached out and covered

Aidan's hand, stilling the fingers that kept clenching into a fist. The rough skin abraded Ethan's, and the hand trembled under his palm. Eventually, Aidan took a deep breath and the vibrations working their way throughout the entirety of his body came to a stop.

Taking a breath himself, Ethan took a chance and pushed. "But what, Aidan? What happened when you told your mother?"

Aidan looked up, and too much brightness shone in his eyes. "She asked me if I'd ever touched Dev."

Ethan's eyelids slid closed for a moment, and he slumped against his chair. "Oh, God, Aidan. She didn't."

"She did." Aidan nodded, his face grim. "She apologized for the accusation, but that was her gut instinct when I told her I was in love with another boy."

"Damn it," Ethan uttered softly. "I'm so sorry."

Aidan shrugged, but his entire body looked strung tight. "Yes, well, she may have decided I wasn't a child molester, but she still didn't want her two young, impressionable children to see their brother being affectionate with another man. They looked up to me, she'd said, and she didn't want my 'gay lifestyle' to influence their choices. She also promised me that my father wouldn't allow any contact with Maddie or Dev at all, if he found out about it."

Ethan's mind conjured a picture of Aidan's dad, a man bigger in stature than Aidan was even today. He'd had very few words, kind or otherwise, for anyone around him. Repressed didn't even begin to describe the man. Ethan shuddered at the memory. "Yeah, I can believe that."

"I believed it too." Looking bleak, Aidan said, "Jesus, Ash, I thought for sure I would have my mother's approval when you and I made those plans to be together. I'd graduated from high school, I had a job, and I was starting to get my brother to trust me again." Devlin had withdrawn from Aidan after his troubles in Texas, showing anger and fear that the oldest sibling had messed everything up and made them move away from their home. "Even little Maddie worshipped her big brother Aidan..." Dejection showed through in the slump of Aidan's shoulders. "Without my mom on my side, all of that would have disappeared forever. She told me if I went to stay with my Uncle Winston in Arizona, and if I got a job and stayed out of trouble, she would bring Dev and Maddie to visit for a few weeks a couple of times a year. My dad didn't like Uncle Winston, so she knew he would never come with them when she brought them to visit. She told me she knew she couldn't control who I chose to be with but that she could decide not to bring Maddie and Dev to see me if she discovered I was out and open in a gay relationship."

Aidan abruptly scooped up the crumpled napkin and took it to the trash. He continued on, his voice rough and low. "For me, her stipulations were as good as controlling who I was with. That meant I could choose you, and lose my brother and sister, or I could go away and have them in my life, at least a little bit. Knowing I didn't want anyone but you made my time living in Arizona easy -- at least in regard to not doing anything that would get those visits taken away from me. It was damn hard being away from you."

So many things raced through Ethan's mind, and he had no idea where to begin. Right now, his half-hard cock and hungry ass could only focus on one thing: *all this time apart and Aidan had never been with another man.* Was that really what he'd just admitted to?

Then something else occurred to Ethan that got him to his feet. "Wait a minute." He spun Aidan around as the beginnings of a new fire stoked in his belly. "Your mom died more than two years ago. Why didn't you come home to her funeral and claim your brother and sister," he choked on the need he couldn't stamp down any longer, "and *me*, then?"

"Because I was scared, damn it! For a thousand reasons, not the least of which was that I figured by that point I'd stayed away for too long and lost you forever anyway. I knew you'd be angry as hell at how I left, and the more I thought about it the more sure I became that you'd never want to hear my voice or see my face again. I'd resigned myself to knowing I would never get over you, and that I would never see you again, but fuck, I never stopped loving you. My chief in Arizona knew I had an interest in becoming a chief myself, and he knew I was from Maine. He heard through upper channels that there would be an opening right here in Redemption. He not only told me about it, he encouraged me to go for it. I stood there in his office and felt like fate had stepped in and given me a second chance to come home and make things right. Before I gave myself a minute to talk myself out of it, I took it."

"Well that was awfully convenient the way fate took over and forced you to make a choice you should have made on your own a long time ago. I guess if Chief Robbins hadn't retired, I'd still be here wondering what happened and why the hell you ran away. It's not good enough, Aidan. You could have done more. You could have contacted me, but you didn't."

Aidan's back went up, stiff with defensiveness. "You know what? It wasn't all about you, Ethan. I had my relationship with my brother and sister to consider in every choice I made too. Maddie was only fifteen when my mother died. My dad could have refused to let her see me if he'd found out about you and me, or even just that I was gay, period." Aidan grasped Ethan's shirt where it lay against his stomach and held on tight. "Don't you see? It wouldn't matter if Maddie didn't care. He was the parent and legal guardian back then. He could have taken her away."

"He could still do that now," Ethan said. God, all of this made his head ache, and he didn't need the complication in his life right now. This all just felt like excuses. "She's not eighteen."

"No, but she will be in two months. That's a manageable amount of time, even if it were to get back to Dad that I'm chasing after my best friend." Aidan slid his arms around Ethan's waist, rubbing their stomachs against one another in a way that went right to Ethan's cock. "When Maddie is eighteen, my dad can't do anything. Dev may have guardianship rights over her now, but you can bet your ass if my father discovered I was out of the closet he would yank those rights away in a heartbeat and have Maddie on a plane to Texas before she could say yea or nay. Two months apart, we can all probably live with that. Almost three years would have been too much."

Aidan dipped down and nuzzled his face into Ethan's neck, nipping and kissing the sensitive flesh. Drowning in renewed desire, Ethan tilted his head without thinking twice, giving Aidan better access to his flesh. He didn't know how he could have missed this so much, when he'd truthfully only had it for one afternoon. But for Ethan, it was as if Aidan's touch pulled him out of a coma … a long, thirteen-year coma, where he'd spent part of almost every day wondering what in the hell he'd done wrong to deserve being abandoned by the only man he'd ever loved. Ethan had wasted so much time on pain that hadn't even been necessary; pain Aidan could so easily have taken away.

"Wait, wait." Ethan shoved Aidan off him as his blood began to heat again. This time it didn't have anything to do with this man's lips, or tongue, or cock. Aidan tried to grab him again, but Ethan batted his hands away and danced out of his range. His chest heaving, he pointed a finger at Aidan, demanding that his arm stay steady. "All you had to do was give me one phone call, damn it. One phone call to explain to me how everything went to shit and that we couldn't be together after all. One phone call to tell me that I hadn't done anything to turn you off and run you out of town. Just one call to tell me I hadn't made a fool out of myself on graduation day, and that you weren't off somewhere with a woman laughing at the nerdy kid with a puppy dog crush." Ethan blinked rapidly to keep the moisture away, and drew his hand into a fist to hide the tremor. "One phone call, damn you, to tell me that you loved me, and that it might be a long time, but eventually we would be together. That's all you had to do."

"I couldn't!" Aidan's cry rose loud enough to rouse the overnight crew. He immediately looked to the door. After a prolonged pause, he leaned into Ethan and whispered heatedly, "I couldn't call you and risk it. Don't you see how we are together? Good Christ, Ash, I was home for one week, you were mad at me, yet with all of our history I was still down on my knees sucking your cock until you came. And I've learned quite a damn bit about self-control over the last dozen years, so it's not like I don't know how to deny myself the things I want. I would bet you've learned to master your self-control too. Yet there you were, knowing you were pissed at me, but holding my head over your dick, just the same, moaning as I gave you a blow job good enough to make you come. What the hell do you think would have happened if I'd gotten in contact with you at any point before now? If I'd been eighteen years old, hell, even twenty or twenty-five, and I'd heard your voice, or come home and crossed paths with you, I would have gone right back to how we were that day by the creek. I would have given up a relationship with my brother and sister in order to be with you. Now I'm sorry if you don't fucking think that's a compelling enough reason for walking away the way I did, or that you think I should have risked it and tried explaining my reasons to you. I would just ask you to consider what you would have done if it meant losing Wyn." Aidan sucker punched Ethan with his raw delivery. The force of his voice pushed Ethan back into the counter, with Aidan right there in his face. "Think about that, about not having the relationship with your brother that you do today. Take a good long look in the mirror and ask yourself if you would have done any different than me."

"I-I…"

The shuffle of bare feet broke the tension between the men. A moment later Devlin and Pete filled the doorway, their bleary-eyed stares taking in the scene in the kitchen.

Dev took an extra step forward, the sleepiness clearing from his stare. "Everything okay?" he asked. His glance moved from Aidan to Ethan, and then back to Aidan. "Aidan?" Ethan swore the younger man looked poised to jump in and defend his brother.

Aidan straightened, giving Ethan some breathing room -- although it wasn't much. He spoke to Dev and Pete, but he kept the intensity of his stare right on Ethan. "No problem. Just a difference of opinion." Aidan's jaw ticked at the back, and he finally took a large step away. "But I guess we've hashed it out as much as is gonna matter. Might as well get some rest." His focus dropped to the counter. He shook his head, and when his gaze came back up, the hard line of his lips and the swirl of banked emotion in his eyes pulled a sucking pain out of Ethan's chest. "Enjoy your pizza."

Aidan pushed away from the counter and slid past the other two men without another word.

After a moment of going back and forth, obvious questions in their eyes, Devlin and Pete said their goodnights and left too.

Ethan stood there in the firehouse kitchen staring at leftover pizza, more exhausted, uncertain, confused, and torn about what he wanted, and *needed*, than ever.

CHAPTER SIX

Aidan's sneakers pounded into the sidewalk in a punishing pace, but he continued to push the speed and length of his daily run, needing the temporary exhaustion that would follow. The tiredness and inability to think wouldn't last much longer than the length of a shower and a meal but Aidan would take whatever the hell he could get.

Anything to take his mind off Ethan and the way the man had pushed Aidan away after his confession at the firehouse.

The rejection burned hot in Aidan's belly, stronger than the exertion he put on his muscles with the extra hard run. He hadn't exactly expected Ethan to forgive and forget everything at the drop of a hat, but at that same time, he thought Ethan might be more understanding of the terrible choice Aidan had been forced to make all those years ago.

Ethan's less than sympathetic reaction crept fingers of doubt into Aidan's thoughts, making him wonder if he had done the right thing after all. Maybe he should have stood up to his mother's prejudice and risked losing his brother and sister. *No!* Aidan could not have lived with himself if he'd lost Maddie and Dev in the ensuing battle. By keeping his nose to the grindstone for those two years after being given a second chance to start his life again, Aidan had worked hard to earn Dev and Maddie's faith and trust again -- especially Dev's. There was no way Aidan could have survived losing his siblings. Not even for Ethan.

Growling, Aidan picked up the pace and ran harder, his body screaming in protest of the workout that pushed him well past his three mile a day norm. The neighborhood was quiet this pretty Sunday morning, with most of the residents either sleeping late or off to an early church service. Aidan took advantage of the low humidity and cool breeze that gave him the freedom to run outdoors, losing himself in a way he couldn't achieve on a treadmill.

Just at the last second, Aidan snapped out of his wandering thoughts and stagger-stepped, barely sidestepping stomping his shoe down on a Pomeranian. Spinning out of reach as the little cognac-colored furball yipped a high-pitched bark and tried to take a nip out of his heels, Aidan slowed his pace and started jogging backward.

He glanced up and spotted a blonde woman skipping down

AIDAN AND ETHAN | 91

the front porch of her house to scoop up the animal.

"Sorry!" Aidan lifted his hand in apology. "Didn't see the little guy there. Hope he's okay."

"My apologies, Chief." The woman waved back. "Chester is new and isn't supposed to be outside unattended. Kids!" The lady -- Aidan lived a block over and didn't know her name -- screeched for her children at the top of her lungs. "Come get the dog and say you're sorry for Chester almost biting Chief Morgan!"

"No, no, not necessary." Still running backward, Aidan rounded the corner. "Just remind them to be careful. There are too many ways Chester can get hurt if he's outside by himself." He waved, and turned back around. "Bye."

"I'll tell them you said so, Chief!" the woman said, even as Aidan moved out of her sight. "They'll listen to you. Thanks!"

Chuckling, Aidan turned the corner to his own street ... and skidded to a halt at the sight that greeted his eyes.

Ethan and Kara in an embrace.

Aidan's stomach dropped right down to the ground.

Kara saw him immediately and offered a smile. "Chief, hi."

"Morning, Kara," Aidan murmured. His mouth turned up at the corners, but his whole face felt frozen. He forced his gaze to Ethan's and his lips to move. "Ethan, hello."

Guarded blue eyes met Aidan's, and the arm that had been around Kara's shoulders slid down and rested at the small of her back. "Aidan."

The comfort and familiarity between the two people in

front of him spread through Aidan like wildfire, leaving him sick with jealousy and, equally cutting, envy. Christ, he wanted to be the one rubbing Ethan's shoulder, as Kara did right now. He wanted his skin to come alive under the simplest touch of Ethan's hand at the base of his spine, as Ethan did to Kara right now. Swallowing a curse, Aidan clamped his jaw and looked down, took deep breaths, and did his damnedest to school his features to bland.

But in his mind, oh, Christ, all he could see was the pure pleasure in Ethan's face that night at the cabin, as Aidan went down on him and sucked him off. All he could remember was Ethan's tightly-strung body fighting against the physical joy Aidan pulled out of him with every long, hard drag on his cock. A prick that grew hard because of Aidan, not Kara. Right there on the street, Aidan's mouth filled with saliva at the memory of Ethan kissing him, deeply, full of passion, with a need that matched Aidan's own. How could they both have reveled in that coupling such a short while ago, and yet here Ethan stood, with a woman, as if none of it had ever happened, let alone mattered?

"Chief," Kara's husky feminine voice cut into his thoughts, "you okay? Your face is very red." She let go of Ethan and put the back of her hand to Aidan's cheek, then his forehead. "I think you pushed too hard on your run and overheated yourself. We need to get some liquids in you before you dehydrate."

Aidan found Ethan's gaze over Kara's shoulder. Christ, he wished Ethan would say something, anything, to show he still cared.

"You should listen to Kara," Ethan finally said, his voice even, careful … distant. "She knows what she's talking about."

There was so little emotion in Ethan's tone that Aidan might as well have been a stranger. Less, if that were possible. Pushing down the wave of hurt that made him want to shake Ethan and expose who and what they once were to each other -- *still were, damn it* -- Aidan fought through the need to out them both. He put his focus on Kara, and the very real concern in her eyes. "I'll be sure to get something at home," he promised. "It's just at the end of the block."

"Ah yes." Kara nodded. "The chief's residence. Haven't seen you coming or going yet, but of course I've heard that you moved in."

"Yep. Such as it is." Right there on the street, Aidan cringed at the wallpaper that covered much of the walls in his home. "I guess I don't need much. It'll do."

Kara chuckled. "Let me know if you need anything. This is me." She pointed to the blue house with the white trim behind her. "I don't think yours has ever been used as more than a transition for new guys or visitors to the firehouse. It has to be short on the comforts of home. Let me know if I can be of help."

Aidan's gaze strayed to Ethan's again, his gut twisting at the man's continued silence. Deflating, he said, "Yeah, I will. Thanks." He edged past both of them, holding his breath as he moved into Ethan's circle of body heat.

His shoulder brushed against Ethan's, and Ethan's breath caught, grabbing Aidan's focus and putting it on Ethan's mouth. A firm top lip and a lush lower one beckoned Aidan, and when Ethan's lips parted, revealing the tip of his tongue, Aidan stifled a moan and shifted, leaning into Ethan...

"I got you, I got you, I got you!" A woman stormed out of the house next door with a man hot on her tail, ripping Aidan and Ethan a foot apart, and setting Aidan's heart into a frantic staccato. Aidan's hand went to his chest, trying to calm the racing, as the man tackled the squealing woman and proceeded to kiss her senseless.

"Newlyweds," Kara said, jerking Aidan even more completely back into reality.

Goddamnit. He'd almost kissed Ethan, not only while standing right out in the middle of the street, but in front of the man's *girlfriend*. Kara happened to be a very nice woman, but fucking A, how Aidan wanted her man for his own.

"We should go, Ethan." Kara curled her hand around Ethan's arm with more of that -- *Aidan gnashed his teeth* -- familiarity. "We don't want to be late."

"Right," Ethan said, and let Kara pull him away.

"Me too." Aidan moved a full house away in three strides. "Gotta go get that Gatorade. See you at the firehouse." He didn't wait, and he didn't dare look back. The thought of seeing Ethan and Kara together in yet another way clawed at Aidan's jealousy, insecurity, and uncertainty about what in the hell to do next.

He wanted Ethan. He wanted his best friend back so fucking badly. He wanted to take their friendship to another level, even beyond what they'd already done in Ethan's cabin. He wanted to be out with Ethan. He wanted to be the one with plans for a Sunday morning, no matter what they were. He wanted to be able to hold Ethan's hand, and he wanted to be able to finish what he'd started on that sidewalk thirty seconds ago. He wanted to kiss Ethan, and he didn't want either one of them to care that they did it with an audience.

An audience that included Kara. Aidan's stomach churned at the thought, even as his heart ached for his wish to become a reality. Kara was a nice person who didn't deserve someone deliberately trying to steal her boyfriend. People would get hurt if Aidan pushed to get Ethan back. If he was successful, Kara got her heart broken. If Aidan was wrong and Ethan really didn't want him back, Aidan would unnecessarily hurt two people, and would have to find a way to deal with the crushing defeat that he'd stayed away from Redemption too long and lost Ethan forever.

Aidan growled when faced with his choices. It was too much to hope he could come home again and pick everything right back up, as if thirteen years of living apart hadn't passed by. Living that on Ethan's end apparently included women.

Aidan didn't know what in the hell to do.

———

ETHAN WATCHED AIDAN TAKE THE two steps to his porch in

one leap and disappear inside his house, the man just a blur at the end of the block now. God, Ethan had never been so tongue-tied as when Aidan had rounded the block right into his and Kara's path. Still so unsure what to make of Aidan's confession at the firehouse, Ethan didn't know how to behave around Aidan without all of the questions about why he'd gone away swirling in his mind anymore. That didn't even take into account how Ethan had wanted to push Kara away, as if Ethan had been caught cheating -- *on Aidan* --right there, as the first thing that entered his mind. And then... And then there was the thing that had turned Ethan's mouth to cotton the second Aidan came into view: shorts and a muscle shirt. Good God, the body Aidan Morgan now possessed would tempt a nun to lay down the habit.

"Ethan?" Kara snapped her fingers in front of Ethan's face. "You okay?" Her brow furrowed. "Now you look a little flushed."

The heat suffusing Ethan's face crept down his neck, burning through his flesh hot enough to make his skin feel tight. Questions loomed in Kara's hazel eyes, making them almost look green. *Almost like Aidan's eyes.*

A little half smile touched Kara's lips, one Ethan had come to dread. "Ethan," she practically purred as she moved around the car to the driver's seat, "is there something you want to tell me?"

"Yeah." He slid into the passenger seat and buckled his safety belt. Sliding on his sunglasses, he added, "If you don't get moving, we're going to be late."

She flicked him in the arm with her fingers. "Smartass. Fine, don't tell me. I knew you wouldn't anyway." Kara gave him a telling, almost pitying look. "You never do."

Ethan curled his hands into fists. "That's because there's never anything to tell."

"You mean there's nothing you're willing to tell," Kara said back, no hesitation at all. "There is a difference. A big one."

"Fine. If that's how you want to see it, then go right ahead." Ethan wasn't about to start spilling his guts to Kara, or anyone else, about things that couldn't be changed anyway. He slid his sunglasses down his nose and raised a brow right back at her. "Next time you feel a crying jag coming on, and you decide to share what is upsetting you with me, rather than going to a quiet corner and crying it out on your own, then you come to me and maybe I'll share what's on my mind."

Kara wrapped her hands tightly around the steering wheel, and gave him a good fast glare. She gunned the engine without another word, and Ethan knew he'd made his point.

Ethan slumped in his seat, but as Kara drove down the street, slowing at the stop sign in front of Aidan's house, Ethan's heart beat in triple time, pounding hard enough to hammer a pattern into his chest. He didn't want to do it, but he found his gaze straying to Aidan's front door, hoping to get one more look at Aidan before Kara drove them away.

———

ETHAN LET HIMSELF INTO HIS cabin, tossing his keys on a narrow table by the front door. All through breakfast with Kara and two of her colleagues, and then the couple of hours he'd spent with his mother and Wyn afterward, Ethan couldn't get Aidan out of his head. Hurt at Aidan's leaving all those years ago still lived inside Ethan, sprouting defensiveness as an automatic mode of self-preservation. At the same time, every time Ethan saw Aidan again, especially now that he knew the terrible choice Aidan's mother had forced upon him, Ethan started to remember the past. His history with the man made everything a hundred times more difficult to sort out his new feelings from the old.

Add to that the fact that Ethan hadn't slept much the last two months -- and hardly at all since Aidan had shown back up in Redemption -- and that left Ethan feeling vulnerable and needy, something he hated.

It also left him weak to memories, no matter how hard he tried to fight them...

——

..."I want to build it right here." Ethan confessed his second most secret desire. He shared the private dream with his first secret desire -- Aidan Morgan. "I want it right here because that's my favorite part of the mountain right there," he pointed to a dense copse of birch trees, "and I want to be able to look at it every morning when I wake up, just because it makes me happy to see it." Aidan made Ethan amazingly happy too, but

Ethan didn't dare share that secret. He'd just gotten Aidan to trust and open up to him, he wasn't going to blow it by talking about his feelings for other boys, now centered squarely on his attraction to Aidan.

God, the guy was so fucking hot. Ethan couldn't ever let Aidan know how he felt. He'd lose Aidan forever. Ethan would rather keep his need to touch and kiss Aidan hidden for the rest of his life than risk losing his friend.

But he could let Aidan in on his plans for his future home, his cabin, he intended to build right here on the mountain. "So," dropping down to the ground of the small clearing, he crossed his legs Indian style, "you're not saying anything. What do you think?"

Aidan lowered himself as well, but rolled to his side and rested his head in his hand. "Dude…" He paused and looked down at the ground. Twisting his fingers in a thick tangle of weed-growth, Aidan cursed, but finally brought his gaze up to Ethan's and held it. "I'm not saying anything because I don't want to crush your feelings."

Ethan took the words like an ice pick to the heart. "You don't like it? B-but what about the tall steepled roof that's gonna make the cabin feel airy and open, and twice as big as it actually is." He scrambled onto his knees and started gesturing with his arms and hands, as if he were a carnival worker trying to get the most people to his booth. "What about the nice big front porch, with one of those little pot-belly stoves built right in, so that you can sit outside in the dead of winter when it's snowing and still be warm. And what about the wall that's really a window? One whole entire wall that's just one big window, where you can just lie in bed and look outside at these trees. Doesn't that sound cool to you?"

Aidan shot to his knees too and grabbed Ethan's arms, stilling them. "Ash, it sounds awesome. It already looks like about the coolest thing ever, and I've never even seen it, except in my head." Aidan held Ethan's wrists in the tight manacles of his hands, tingling awareness all up and down Ethan's limbs. "That's not the problem."

Forcing his thoughts off Aidan's electric touch, Ethan eventually processed what Aidan had actually said, and his chest swelled. He furrowed his brow at his friend. "If it sounds so cool, then what's your problem ?"

Aidan gave Ethan's arms a little tug. "Ash, buddy, you're living in a fantasy. You can't just build a house wherever you want. You've got to own the land, and I don't know, but I think land costs a shitload of money."

Just like that, the breath Ethan had been holding released, drawing out an involuntary smile. "Oh, well, that's no big deal." He lifted his hands and pointed all around, bringing Aidan's hold with them. "My mom owns this property. She has since my grandma died."

Aidan's jaw dropped, his hands went lax, and his arms thudded to his sides. "What?"

Ethan chuckled and threw himself down on the ground. Stacking one hand over the other under his head, he shifted and met Aidan's wide-open gaze. "I told you we didn't have to worry about being here and wouldn't get in trouble for it. What did you think I meant by that?"

Aidan closed his mouth, but opened it right back up again as if he were going to speak, only to close it again. Finally, he threw his hands up in the air. "I don't know what I thought. Maybe that Maine owned it or something, and that whoever wanted to come could. Shit, Ash," Aidan lay back down on his side, right beside Ethan, "why didn't you tell me your family was loaded?"

Ethan chuckled. It wasn't like he had any fears that Aidan was his friend because he was cool or had lots of money. If that were the case, Aidan would have been gone after the first week of eating lunch together, when he had surely discovered just how *un-cool* Ethan was. "My family isn't rich," Ethan assured. "We just own this piece of the mountain. My great-grandfather bought it when he moved here and it has been passed down ever since."

Aidan snorted and jabbed Ethan in the shin with his boot. "When you own land, Ashworth, you're rich."

Ethan went all warm inside at how easy Aidan had become around him. "No," he spared the guy a glance and a smile, "when you sell the land you own for a shitload of money, then you might be rich. Right now, my mom just owns land that is potentially worth a lot of money. Since I know she isn't gonna sell it, and neither will Wyn or I when we get it, we're not rich."

Aidan dipped his head. "Yeah, I guess that's a good point."

He suddenly grinned, and the sight of his beautiful smile grabbed Ethan in the heart. "It's kinda cool, you know?" Aidan said. "I think I'd rather own a piece of a mountain than have a big check in the bank."

"Yeah, me too."

"So," Aidan rolled onto his back and poked Ethan in the elbow with a playful nudge, "since you really can build it someday, tell me about your cabin again."

"Okay, well…"

Side by side, lying in the grass, arms folded under their heads, Ethan went over every detail of his cabin. With every idea he revealed, that Aidan grunted with approval or showed outright excitement about, Ethan sent a prayer to God that somehow, someway, Aidan could live in the cabin with him too…

———

…Ethan ran his hand lovingly along the walls of his home, in his mind transferring the groves of the imperfect wood under his palm to the indentations and slopes of Aidan's perfect body. God, he remembered touching Aidan with such discovery on graduation day, and then just three weeks ago, with such pent-up need and frustration, right in this very cabin. Ethan had never thought he would have Aidan in his home, a place that in his teenage dreams he'd put Aidan with him, from the moment they became friends. Almost out of defiance, Ethan had asked his mother for permission to build on the land, and then had a contractor friend help him build the small house. Ethan didn't need it to be big, but rather just what he'd always wanted, even if it came into creation without Aidan.

With every beam Ethan had secured in place, and every nail driven home, to the final touches of furniture or flowers on the front porch, Ethan couldn't stop the dreams that came to him at night when his guard was down; he could not fight the desire he still carried for Aidan Morgan.

Ethan stumbled to the bed and then to the small space of wall between the window seating and his nightstand. Tucking in, as if he could protect himself, Ethan closed his eyes, trying to fight off the visions of him and Aidan as teens, succumbing to each other for the first time under the cover of trees -- trees that stood right outside his picture window, mocking him for the liar he was. Every piece of this home had come together with Aidan on his mind, whether those thoughts were good, bad, or full of righteous rage. And to this day, when he went to bed at night, Ethan still had fevered dreams of a naked Aidan kissing him, sucking him, God, fucking him. Those dreams stirred Ethan's cock and brought on a torrent of wet dreams.

Ethan opened his eyes and stared out the window, but all he could see was Aidan amongst the trees. First as a sixteen-year-old with guarded hope in his beautiful eyes, to a laugh finally shining in that gaze when he'd let Ethan become his friend. The picture then shifted to lust swirling dark in those pale green depths as he and Ethan jerked each other off while exposing their bodies and their hearts. Just as quickly as Ethan admired the Aidan of his past, the phantom image of the teen standing on the other side of the glass morphed into the Aidan from this morning, all hot and sweaty, half naked in shorts and a shirt with the sleeves cut off.

Then, his eyes on Ethan, as if he could see him, Aidan drew the shirt off over his head and tossed it to the ground, unearthing a stunning chest with a thin line of hair that mapped a trail straight down to the waistband of his shorts … and beyond.

Ethan's gaze blurred as his focus followed that fine line of dark hair, and his cock came to life right where he stood. He couldn't hold back the moan as he reached down and rubbed himself through his khaki pants, all with his stare glued on something he knew wasn't real, but at the same time he couldn't make disappear.

Aidan not only seemed to watch Ethan from twenty-five feet away, but his sexy-as-hell voice got into Ethan's head, urging him onward. "Take off your shirt and pants, baby. I want to see everything."

As if he didn't control them at all, Ethan's hands came up and worked the top button on his shirt open, and then another, and another, until no more remained. Aidan nodded, and Ethan shrugged out of his shirt, letting it drift to the hardwood floor in silence. He moved down to his belt, but his heart raced out of control and his breathing grew erratic. Ethan paused.

"Show me, Ash." Aidan stuck his own hand down his shorts and rubbed. "I know you're hard. I am too. Open your pants, baby. Let me see your cock."

Ethan's prick pushed against the fabric of his khakis, and his balls swelled and became weighty between his thighs, already begging for release. Ethan rolled his shoulder against the wall and reached for his belt, working the buckle open while he stared at the mirage of Aidan through narrowed eyes. Ethan watched Aidan play with himself while Ethan revealed his cock, all with Aidan's hand still concealed behind his shorts.

Ethan pushed his pants and underwear down just enough to get his erection free. He immediately took the rigid length in his hand and started to stroke himself slowly. "Show me too," Ethan whispered, his throat raw with wanting as he stared at Aidan, so far away, yet so completely inside his head. "I want to see everything too."

"I'll give you whatever you want." Aidan toed off one running shoe and sock, then the other. "You know that."

"Yeah." Ethan stared, riveted, pulling his dick in an over-handed drag from base to tip, making himself hurt with a too-hard yank on dry skin. Without looking away, he fumbled in the drawer of his nightstand, his fingers grazing over a hard, thick rod, to a soft, cool-to-the-touch bottle of lube.

"Get 'em both, baby," Aidan instructed. "You're gonna need them."

Outside the cabin, Aidan pulled down his shorts, revealing a firm cock sticking upward from a nest of dark curls. Everything but that vision flew from Ethan's mind. He only managed to get a small dollop of lube on his fingers before he groaned and started jerking off, trying to get in tandem with Aidan's pulls. Aidan made a growling noise too and double-fisted the length of his cock, replacing one drag right after the other, never leaving an inch of his cock free for more than a second. Ethan writhed against the wall at his back, jerking on his cock with one hand and playing with his nipples with the other, twisting and tugging the tiny hardening tips, making them just as aching and needy as the rest of his body.

"Oh Christ, baby, you feel so fucking good." Aidan's skin pulled taut over his face. He pumped his hips in big jerks, shoving his cock into both of his hands. "Tight. So tight. Tell me you can feel me inside your hot ass."

Ethan shook his head, even as he couldn't tear his eyes away or stop stroking his cock. His voice rough, he uttered, "Can't."

"You can."

Ethan knew what Aidan wanted. More, what Ethan needed. God, he needed Aidan to take him, to consume him in every way, to steal him away from his life for just five minutes with a promise that he would be safe. Yes, oh yes, how Ethan wanted all of that.

He turned to the side against the wall, and then faced into it, pressing his cheek against the knotted wood. Still looking out the window, he reached for the thick wand and slicked it up with the leftover lube on his hand.

"Do it," Aidan said softly, but with command, watching so, so closely as Ethan slipped the rod between his legs and fitted the tip against his hole. "Please, Ash..." They both grunted, and it was almost as if the rounded end of the anal probe was Aidan's cock, and the man could feel it pushing against Ethan's pucker, nudging hard to break through. "Do it. Let me fuck you."

Frantic for everything Aidan wanted, Ethan bore down on the solid length and pushed it up hard against his entrance, groaning at the pulling of his ring. "Make me feel it, Aidan," Ethan begged. His eyes slid closed with the next bout of insistent pressure on his bud. "Goddamn, make me feel you... Oh!" *Right then*, Ethan shoved the wand home, the length tearing through his ass and unbearably stretching his chute. "Ohhh fuck..."

And suddenly Aidan was no longer outside, but instead behind Ethan inside the cabin, pounding him into the wall with the force of his fucking. Ethan swore he felt the grit and sweat from Aidan's run still on the man's body, smearing into Ethan's flesh with the weight of Aidan on his back. Aidan took Ethan hard and without quarter, filling Ethan's ass to the hilt with every slam of his cock into Ethan's body, circling and grinding there before pulling away, only to take him somehow deeper with the next full stroke.

With his hand still wrapped around his cock, Ethan pulled hard on his prick, gasping and wincing with the sensations of a dick in his ass and a hand job, both at the same time. Plastered against the wall, with little room to move or struggle away from what his body forced him to feel, Ethan panted, churned his hips, and squeezed his screaming channel around the invasion in his ass.

"Oh yeah." Aidan chanted at Ethan's ear, his hot breath snaking down Ethan's neck and causing a shiver. "Come for me, baby. Come right now." He put his arm around Ethan's chest and bore them both into the wall under his crushing weight. Inside Ethan's mind, Aidan's voice, body, very being, took Ethan over completely. "I only come with you."

Aidan forced his other hand down onto Ethan's cock and pulled painfully hard on Ethan's erection. At the same time, he tucked deep into Ethan's ass, consuming Ethan in every way. Ethan couldn't fight the need. With a hoarse shout, he pumped his dick right against the wall and came. His rectum contracted around Aidan's thick penis with every spurt of ejaculate painted onto the wood, the two needs tied together, one spurring the other to a stronger, more complete release than Ethan had ever experienced in his life.

Firm lips brushed in Ethan's hair, and a whisper of, "You look beautiful when you come," caressed his ear. The weight disappeared from Ethan's back, and the long, wonderful cock slid out of his ass, drawing a hiss and a curling of Ethan's toes in his shoes. Ethan spun quickly, but, of course, he was alone.

No big, hard, naked Aidan inside his cabin, grinning after just giving Ethan the fucking of his life. Ethan looked to the window, but Aidan no longer stood outside against the backdrop of their mountain either.

Still, the warmth that had engulfed Ethan moments ago remained, cloaking him with the man's presence, leaving Ethan feeling safe, as if Aidan really had been inside this cabin. As if there was a certainty he would be back.

From the moment Ethan had seen the mirage of Aidan outside, his exhaustion had gone away. Even though the fantasy had passed, Ethan didn't feel the heaviness on his shoulders that seemed to rule much of his life these days. He knew it would return, but maybe if he closed his eyes and thought of Aidan again, he could keep it at bay, for a time.

Ethan thought about the pain in Aidan's eyes when sharing the story of why he'd gone away, and a flicker of forgiveness *tap tap tapped* against his chest, requesting entry.

As he slid to the floor, Ethan just didn't know if he could open himself up to that kind of potential heartache again and answer Aidan's knock.

Chapter Seven

Aidan rapped his knuckles against the front door of the familiar house, praying like hell he had his information correct.

Christ, he didn't want Ethan to know he was here.

The door swung open, and shock registered on Wyn's rough-looking face. "Aidan. Hi." Wyn glanced all around the darkness of the front yard beyond, as if he expected to find answers looming behind Aidan. "What can I do for you? Ahh, Ethan's not here, if that's who you're looking for."

"Nope. Umm…" *Shit, I knew the woman; I have every right to be here.* "I came to say hello to your mom, if that's okay?"

Wyn's dark eyes widened. To his credit, he didn't slam the door in Aidan's face. *Of course, he doesn't know I walked away from his brother after planning a life together either.*

"Oh, well, I guess that would be fine," Wyn answered. "She likes having visitors and she seems to be okay today."

"I already told you once that I'm not deaf, son!" Jayne bellowed from inside the house. "Now let the boy in already!"

Wyn smiled and shook his head. "See? As I was about to tell you, before I was *so rudely interrupted,*" he turned his head and raised his voice, "she's up for company tonight, and to go right in!" Wyn's gaze suddenly narrowed in the direction of the driveway. "Why in the hell is your sister sitting in the truck?"

Aidan followed Wyn's stare to Maddie, where she sat in the passenger seat of his vehicle. Maddie looked up, saw the men staring at her, and waved as she made a funny face. Aidan chuckled. His sister was something else. "She doesn't really know your mother and she didn't want to look like she was gawking or intruding. I just picked her up from work, and we're going to eat afterward, so she said she would wait in the truck."

"There's no point in her sitting in the truck in the dark." Wyn pushed past Aidan to the walkway. "You go on in and say hi. I'm sure you remember how to find the living room. I'll grab your sister and bring her inside. She can at least share a drink with me while you visit."

"Hey." Aidan whipped out his hand and grabbed Wyn before he got any farther away. Wyn turned back to look at him, and Aidan said, "She's seventeen. No alcohol."

"Are you kidding me?" Wyn asked, his voice rising. "I'm

not going to sit in my mother's kitchen and drink beers with a teenager. She's just a kid."

Aidan couldn't help his mind drifting to the teasing Wyn had directed at Maddie a few weeks ago at the firehouse, or the way Maddie had glared back at him with fire in her eyes. "That's right, she is still a kid." Aidan couldn't help the lecturing tone that slipped into his voice. "And you're what, a few years younger than Dev, if I remember correctly. That puts you around twenty-three or so?"

Wyn nodded. "Yeah."

"That's good that you're making note of the difference in your ages. Don't be forgetting it."

Wyn snorted. He looked horrified at the very concept of finding Maddie attractive. "Yeah. That's not gonna be a problem, Chief. She's getting a glass of tea or a soda, and that's it. I'm a cop. I've got no interest in corrupting a minor."

Aidan took a good hard look at Wyn and didn't see the younger man trying to evade eye contact. Abruptly, Aidan backed off. "Glad to hear it." He stepped inside the house. "Thank you for letting me visit with your mother. I won't stay long."

Aidan watched as Wyn shoved his hands into his pockets and walked to the truck. The young man held back a respectable distance, very politely knocked on the closed window, and Aidan decided to trust the Wyn. He headed inside but when he reached the arch that led to the living room, his legs suddenly locked in place. He remembered everything about this house.

It reeked of memories of Ethan, and sent tingles of awareness down his spine. At the same time, nothing about the place looked the same, and that washed a sense of loss over Aidan that weakened his knees.

Buck up, man. It has been thirteen years. The house looking different doesn't automatically mean Ethan has changed completely too.

"Come on in." Jayne's voice reached him from inside the room, and got his feet moving again. "I won't bite. I promise."

Aidan rounded the sofa and found a petite woman with an elfin face and dark hair lying on the couch. She had two pillows propping her partially upright and a big dog sleeping on her blanket-covered legs.

A smile turned up the corners of Aidan's mouth at seeing this woman again, and a lightness stole away the heaviness in his heart. "Ah, okay…" He took a seat that put him close to Jayne. "Now you, I remember."

Jayne smiled back, and reached out to pat Aidan's knee. "Yes, the house doesn't look at all the same, I'm afraid." She gave him a good once-over. "You don't look exactly the same yourself, Aidan Morgan."

Aidan's cheeks filled with heat. "No, I guess not. Working as a firefighter all these years has changed me some."

"All that Arizona sunlight has too," she said back quickly. "You've got more color than I remember, and a few lines around your eyes. It's from doing all that squinting, I would imagine."

He touched his hand to the corner of his eye, feeling the

grooves himself. "Maybe. Of course, it could just be from the fact that I'm getting older too."

"Well, aren't we all." Jayne smoothed her hand over the sleek pull of her hair. "Some of us faster than others."

"Are you kidding, Mrs. Ashworth?" Aidan pushed forward to the edge of his chair. "You look fantastic. I'm surprised --" He bit his tongue mid-sentence, mentally kicking himself in the ass for not thinking before he spoke.

The blue of Jayne's eyes softened. She reached out to cover Aidan's hand, giving him a squeeze. "You mean you're surprised by how well I look, considering what you've heard about how sick I am."

Aidan wanted to drop to the floor and crawl under the couch. "I'm sorry. That was insensitive of me."

"It's all right." Her voice was gentle, but sure, and put Aidan back to a place of peace. Sitting there, he recalled one of the two reasons he had loved coming to this house when he was a teenager. Jayne Ashworth. Aidan so, so, wanted the other reason, *Ethan*, back in his life. "And please, call me Jayne," she said. "I'm nobody's Mrs. anymore."

"I've heard about that since coming home. I'm sorry that happened to you and Ethan and Wyn, at what I'm sure was one of the toughest moments of your life."

"Don't be sorry. I'm not." Aidan reared back. Seeing that, Jayne said, "It's true, I swear. Sometimes we let things go for longer than they should, and we don't make a change until something life-altering forces us to see the life we've lived in a new light. My ex-husband and I were not the best of friends when things were good in our marriage. One can't expect something more substantial will suddenly blossom when a crisis arises. That only happens in the movies. In real life, that's when people who were coasting by on fumes end up divorcing. If we'd been good friends from the beginning, we could have weathered it." She grabbed hold of Aidan's attention and held him captive with her stare. She pierced him with one look, and he couldn't break away. "True friends can find their way to each other through anything, and forgive anything, even very big mistakes. Do you see what I'm saying?"

"Umm…" Damn it, what had Ethan told this woman about his and Aidan's relationship? Feeling his way around in the dark, Aidan responded, "I hope you're right." The constant hurt and hostility that radiated off Ethan every time Aidan got within two feet of him assaulted Aidan right there in the living room and clamped a tight squeeze on his throat. "Sometimes the hurt is too big, though, and people can't get past their own pain to see the view from the other side." Christ, time and again, as it had done a million times since leaving Redemption, frissons of self-doubt entered Aidan's thoughts, weakening his resolve. "Maybe even the tightest bond of friendship can't weather some storms. Maybe sometimes, no matter how much you want it, things aren't meant to be." He looked into blue eyes that so reminded him of another set. These eyes were full of awareness and empathy, and Aidan swore he looked right into Ethan's heart and begged him for answers. "The thing is, how do you know when to push and when to let go?"

Wham! The slam of a door rattled the pictures on the walls. Seconds later, Ethan stormed into the living room with Wyn and Maddie hot on his tail.

His cheeks ruddy and his blond hair mussed, Ethan screeched to a stop. He turned a storming gaze on Aidan. "What are you doing here, Morgan?"

"Ethan," Jayne reproached.

Overstepping Jayne's voice, Aidan uttered, "Shit," and shot to his feet. Taking Ethan in, after being so close to baring his soul to the very man's mother, Aidan's throat went bone dry. "I-I thought you had a volley ball game tonight."

"The other team forfeited the game when they didn't show." Ethan spoke each word through clenched teeth. "I sent the girls home and thought I'd stop in to say hi to my mother before heading home myself. Imagine my surprise when I saw your truck in the drive."

"I-I … It's nothing." Christ, the heat of guilt swamped Aidan, and he didn't know why. He hadn't done anything wrong. *Not in this decade anyway*, the voice of doubt crept in, haunting him. "I just wanted to say hi to your mom."

"Yet you obviously made a point of coming when you knew I wouldn't be here."

"It wasn't like that," Aidan said.

At the same time, Jayne hissed, "Ethan Ashworth," in one of those foreboding "mother" tones.

"To think I almost --" Ethan stopped, pursing his lips tight.

Aidan took a step closer, his heart thudding hard, pushing to fight another day. "You almost what, Ash?"

Ethan looked at his mother and came back to Aidan. "Nothing." Frost covered a layer over the one word. "Not a damn thing."

"But…"

Maddie suddenly pushed past both Wyn and Ethan. "I think we should go, bro. *Right now.*" Wrapping her hand around Aidan's arm, she started pulling him toward the door. "Sorry, ma'am," she called over her shoulder in Jayne's direction. "I'm Maddie, by the way. Aidan's sister. Nice to meet you. Have a good night."

"Nice to meet you too, sweetheart," Jayne replied, her tone sing-songy, so different from just a moment ago.

Maddie kept tugging on Aidan, but her step faltered when she reached the blockade of Wyn. "Later, Ashworth."

"Doubtful, M & M," Wyn teased as he stepped aside with a flourish. "Have fun in school tomorrow."

Maddie gave the young man a narrow-eyed, deadly look as she dragged Aidan behind her. "Asshole," she muttered under her breath.

"Maddie," Aidan admonished, his voice hushed.

"What?" She threw Aidan a mean look too. "He is one. Or, he acts like one half the time, anyway," she amended.

Strong fingers dug into Aidan's other arm. He swung around, prepared to apologize to Wyn for Maddie's remark. Instead he found himself looking into a fire sparking Ethan's eyes to life.

Ethan tore his focus away for a second and put it on Maddie. "Can you give us two minutes, Maddie? I'd appreciate it."

"Uh, sure." Maddie let go of Aidan and pointed behind her. "I'll just wait for you in the truck." The eyes she turned on Aidan were full of questions. "Is that okay?"

Aidan gave a clipped nod. "I'll be fine. We'll go eat in a minute. All right?"

"Okay. Sure." Shoving her hands into her zipper sweater, she made fast tracks to the truck and climbed inside.

Both men waited until they heard the click of the door closing, and then spun and got in each other's faces.

"I didn't mean anything --"

"You had no right --"

They both snapped their mouths shut in unison, and each looked ready to burst at the seams.

Aidan took one very deliberate step away from the belligerent man in front of him, before the heat of Ethan's emotions accidentally set him ablaze. He stamped down his instinct to defend himself and forcibly modulated his voice. "I apologize." Taking yet another step back, he locked his legs and clasped his hands behind his back in a military stance. "Go ahead. What did you want to say?"

Ethan opened his mouth, but just as quickly closed it again. As he stood there in prolonged silence, the rigidity went out of his frame, and a murkiness took over his eyes. Aidan stared, his heart cracking as he watched *life* leave a person's body. Ethan's body. The only man he had ever loved.

"Jesus, man." Aidan took a step forward.

"No." Ethan's hands went up in front of his chest in a flash, warding Aidan off. "Don't you dare pity me. Not right now." His voice broke like an adolescent, tearing at Aidan even harder. "I wouldn't be able to take it." He turned on a dime and walked to the door, leaving Aidan standing there on the sidewalk, aching to help, but knowing his hands were tied.

Ethan stopped at the threshold, but didn't turn around. He reached out and grabbed the doorframe, and the shadows lit him with the silhouette of a physically strong body that didn't know how to hold itself upright. "You just...You should have consulted me before you came here. You had no right."

Aidan took a fast step forward but then stopped himself before advancing another step and taking Ethan into his arms. Ethan had repeatedly said he didn't want the comfort, so Aidan forced his hands to his sides.

"I just wanted to say hello to her, E, I swear." Aidan curled his hands into fists so that he didn't caress Ethan's back. "Your mom was always kind to me, and I felt like I owed her a visit. I tried to come when you weren't here because I didn't want you to think I was looking for a way to bump into you, or use the visit to manipulate you. I just wanted to come, see her, and leave, with no fuss. I promise."

"Fine then." Rust seemed to coat each word that left Ethan's mouth. "I'm sorry I snapped. Your sister is waiting. You should go."

"Okay. If that's what you want." Hating to do it, going against every instinct he felt in his gut, Aidan walked to his truck and left Ethan standing there, alone.

Ethan closed the door and leaned into it, his heart racing so fast it tingled numbness in all of his extremities. God, why wouldn't Aidan just go away and let Ethan slip back into the routine he'd constructed for himself so long ago; one that let him get through his days without constant pain and hurt; one that worked out so well because he didn't let himself *feel* too much of anything.

So much for thinking Aidan might act as a soothing balm on his tired soul. The man hadn't brought comfort just now, that was for damn sure. Ethan had just wanted to shove the man out and shield his mother from gawkers, even if they thought they were sincere. When he saw Aidan's truck in the drive, he'd acted on instinct and jumped in to protect. Ethan just wanted one person in his life not to hurt as he did.

The blow of losing Aidan at eighteen, when he'd been so sure they would last forever, to then thinking he would lose his mother a year later, to *actually* losing his father when the asshole couldn't stand up and be a man for his wife and family... *Good God.* Ethan had discovered that shutting down allowed him to function and do the things needed every day in order to survive.

Only now, here Aidan was, showing up in practically every

part of Ethan's life, and infecting the routine he had perfected so long ago. Making him *feel*, making him *want*, making him *need* another person again.

No, Ethan assured himself as he straightened, *I don't need him. I don't.* He took half a dozen deep breaths, and when he felt more like himself, opened his eyes.

His brother stood waiting for him. It was clear in the way Wyn studied him that he had witnessed Ethan's conversation with Aidan, as well as the private moment he'd just taken to get himself back under control.

Wyn broke the silence first. "For what it's worth, I believe Aidan. He only came to say hi to Mom. I didn't read any ulterior motives in his eyes or demeanor, and you know I never would have let him inside if I thought he was using her to manipulate you."

Ethan unclenched his hands, spread his fingers, and once again counted to ten. "It's fine, Wyn. I'm fine."

Wyn glanced toward the living room, cursed under his breath, and took three steps forward until barely a foot separated the brothers. He lowered his voice considerably, but looked Ethan dead-on in the eyes. "You're in love with Aidan."

All of the air sucked right out of Ethan's lungs. He grabbed the doorknob before his legs went out from under him. "Wh-wh…" He wheezed and drew back until his head cracked against the door. He wanted to look away, but couldn't break the hold of his brother's dark eyes. Clearing his throat, he tried again. "What did you say?"

"And it's more than that, isn't it?" Wyn went on speaking under his breath, as if Ethan had never said a word. "He's in love with you too, isn't he?" Ethan opened his mouth while shaking his head, but Wyn put a clamp on it with his hand. "No, don't even attempt to deny it. I saw the way he looked at you just now, like it killed him to hear you question his motives for being here. Even with that hurt, I saw him move to comfort you, but then stop himself from doing it."

Oh God, oh God, oh God. Ethan reeled. *Wyn knows everything.* His younger brother always was good at watching and picking up clues, and he did like to poke his nose in where it didn't belong. That was probably what would take him from a rookie cop to detective and then chief, in record time. Damn it. Why couldn't he have had an idiot for a brother?

Ethan did a mental search through story after story that might justify and explain what Wyn had witnessed.

"I can see you trying to spin something like you're showing me a movie script," Wyn shared, his voice low. "Don't even bother trying to lie to me. You're gay."

Fuck. The timing sucked, but Ethan could see Wyn knew the score. His brother had figured him out. How many other people would too, as soon as they saw Aidan and Ethan in the same room together?

Looking at Wyn, Ethan asked, "Are you disgusted?"

"Yes," his brother replied, punching Ethan in the gut with that one crushing word. Wyn's brown eyes deepened with emotion to almost pure black. "I'm disgusted by the fact that you have someone…" Wyn stopped for a few seconds as his voice wavered. He cleared his throat and stiffened his lip. "You have someone right there within your grasp, someone who can help you deal with what's going on with Mom, and what will happen in the not too distant future." Wetness filled Wyn's eyes, but he swiped it away with the backs of his hands without stopping. "But for whatever reason you're pushing him away, just like you do with everybody, even Kara. Although, Christ, I guess now I know why you guys never seemed particularly in love with each other, even at the beginning. Fuck this, E. Are you afraid to come out? Are you afraid of what people will say if you're with another man? Because if you are, get over it. That's just pussy of you."

Anger renewed the strength in Ethan's legs. He pushed away from the door and shoved Wyn against the hallway wall. "First, you don't know what it will feel like to have people staring at you when they realize you're sexually attracted to other men, so don't tell me to get over it. Second," he put a hand to his brother's chest, held him there, and continued in a furious whisper, "you also don't know the first thing about the circumstances of what went down between me and Aidan, so don't assume I'm a pussy for not falling into his arms the second he came back to town."

"I don't give a shit why you're mad at him." Snapping his arms up between them, Wyn chopped Ethan's arms and quickly broke out of the hold. He executed a fast move and in two ticks had Ethan up against the wall in a forceful hold.

So much tangible emotion coiled in Wyn that his voice came out in a low, rough growl. "Our mother is about as ill as a person can get while still drawing breath on this earth, and it is going to wreck our lives when she is gone. I don't have one damn person who wants to hold me and take care of me when that day comes. But you, man, you do, I can see it. Yet you're gonna walk away from it and choose to go through this alone. That makes me sick. What if it wasn't Mom who was ill, huh? What if it was Aidan? What if in ten years, or even twenty, you find out he has cancer? Or forget that, what if he dies in a fire tomorrow? Will you stand over his grave and feel satisfied with yourself because you held your ground when he made a mistake, that whatever it was, he is clearly sorry for having made? Do you want to be in Mom's shoes in thirty years and not have Aidan in your life, holding your hand, loving you as much then as he so obviously does now? Is that who you want to be, brother? Because that's not the guy I always looked up to. That's not the man I emulated and hoped to become one day myself."

Ethan's chest burned and he had trouble breathing. Everything he had stuffed down to this point in his life punched and shoved inside him, fighting to get free and drown him. *No.* He couldn't let it happen. Panic raced through him, and he knew he wouldn't survive the flood.

Barely able to talk, Ethan grabbed his brother's forearms and squeezed. "You don't understand. It's not that simple."

Wyn dug his fingers into Ethan's shoulders, forcing him

to *feel.* "Yes," the one word from Wyn punctured Ethan like a bullet, "it is."

Ethan pulled against Wyn's hold, and the brothers struggled against the power in each other in a modified fight. They didn't exchange words, but the rage of emotions in both men, that in their own way they each fought not to show, infused them with incredibly focused strength.

"Not giving in," Wyn promised, his voice harsh.

Ethan twisted and shoved, getting his brother back up against the wall. "Me," he side-stepped a kick to his knees, "either."

Thud.

Woof! Woof! Woof!

The clack of canine toenails on hardwood floor echoed in the house like hail on a tin roof. Oz charged at Ethan and Wyn from the living room, jumping on them as he barked up a storm.

Both men broke apart in a flash. Ethan got his dog off them and rushed to the living room, Wyn almost right on top of him.

They found Jayne Ashworth lying crumpled on the floor.

Ethan banged on the front door of the little house, unsure what time it was, or even what day it was any longer. All he knew was that he didn't feel human anymore, and he didn't have any control over a damn thing around him, or how to get it back. When he got a glimpse of himself in his rearview mirror a few minutes ago, he hadn't even recognized the face that looked back at him, even though logically he knew he must look the same, as the people at the hospital recognized him only minutes before he'd climbed behind the wheel of his car.

Fucking shit. Where the hell are you? Ethan slammed his fist into the wood again, scraping it raw with the force of his hits. *I don't know anywhere else to go. I can't think of any other names of people or recognize any houses except yours.*

"Oh, God." Ethan dug his fingers into his hair and pulled, spinning in a circle. He looked through the darkness at all of the quiet surrounding homes, and prayed for divine intervention. He didn't understand it, but nothing looked familiar -- except this house. He knew this front door. "What am I supposed to do? Think, Ashworth, think. Go home. Where do you live?"

Oh God, I don't know where I live.

"I'll just drive." He turned to head back to his car. He'd known what his vehicle looked like and where to find it in the parking lot. As he turned, the scrape of metal reached his ears, and the door behind him opened.

A gravelly voice, one he *knew*, reached Ethan's ears. "Ash?" Ethan spun on that beloved nickname.

Aidan. Oh, it's Aidan.

Aidan stepped onto the porch, flannel pajama bottoms on, and nothing else. *He's beautiful*, Ethan remembered that. Aidan reached out and cupped Ethan's jaw, and Ethan knew that callused touch too. *He's my home. I'm home.*

"It's five o'clock in the morning, man," Aidan said. "Are you okay?"

"I need you," Ethan whispered roughly. He grabbed Aidan around the neck and crushed their lips together in a hard kiss.

CHAPTER EIGHT

Aidan moaned, and he stumbled under the force of Ethan's kiss. The man pushed his tongue against the seam of Aidan's lips, demanding entry, and, *Oh Christ*, Aidan opened up and let him inside. Ethan devoured Aidan with the invasion and dug his hands into Aidan's back, scraping over Aidan's flesh with chewed-down fingernails, making Aidan shiver. Lust and long-denied need took hold of Aidan and had him reaching for the waistband of Ethan's jeans and yanking out his shirt, wanting to get his hands on the body he had dreamed about for too many years.

He forced his hands under the fabric to a taut waist and tore at the buttons, ripping the shirt down Ethan's arms, baring the fucking sexiest chest he had ever seen in his life. The man's tan body begged for a full exploration, and his copper nipples twisted to tiny points, reaching for a touch. Growling and uncaring that he stood on his front porch, Aidan bowed Ethan over his arm and lowered his mouth for a taste of his flesh.

The salty flavor of perspiration burst over Aidan's taste buds, and the hard tip of Ethan's nipple scraped against his tongue. Ethan dove his fingers into Aidan's hair, clamping a hold on his scalp as he uttered, "Oh God, yes … yes. Need more." He pulled Aidan off his chest and grabbed him around the waist in a tight hold. Forcing Aidan to walk backward, Ethan pushed them inside, pausing only long enough to kick the door closed with his foot. "Want you." The confession escaped Ethan in a low rush, the breath of it washing over Aidan's lips and going into his mouth. Ethan bit at Aidan's mouth, hard enough to sting and probably leave a mark. Almost frantic in his movements, Ethan shoved Aidan in the direction of the hallway and found the door that led to his bedroom, all while remaining locked against his front. "Want your cock." Ethan's voice sounded stripped and strangled. "Want your ass."

Aidan jerked, coming to a stop as the backs of his knees hit the foot of his bed. Immediate suspicion mingled with concern at Ethan's presence and behavior. The few possibilities of why he would show up at this time, like this, all swirled with the pain Aidan felt for Ethan's situation, sending warning bells through his mind.

Tearing himself away from the kiss, Aidan clutched Ethan's head in his hands and forced the man to look at him. The pinpoint pupils, flushed skin, and shallow breathing all sent signals of fear to Aidan's heart. "E?" In response, Ethan lunged for another kiss, and Aidan's muscles strained as he struggled to hold the man a pace away. "What's wrong? Are you okay?"

Ethan clutched at the waistband of Aidan's pajama bottoms, pulled, and got them down around his hips. "I will be as soon as I'm inside you." Urgency guided the man's voice and movements, and he dropped to his knees to take a nipping bite out of Aidan's belly. He finished pushing Aidan's bottoms the rest of the way down, freeing the hard length of Aidan's cock, the heavy weight of arousal making it stick out straight. Ethan dipped down, licked all up and down the firm ridge, and Aidan's prick jumped while his balls squeezed tight with desire.

Oh Jesus, I've wanted this for so damn long.

Just as Aidan prepared himself for the only blowjob he'd ever wanted -- his first -- Ethan spun him around and chopped out his knees, tumbling Aidan face-first onto the bed. Cool sheets chilled Aidan's front, and right away the burn of Ethan's skin and the solid force of male weight covered him from behind. The dig of a belt buckle dented Aidan's leg, and he knew Ethan had shoved his own pants down to mid-thigh. With a small shift, Ethan widened Aidan's legs, and, *Holy Mother*, a hard-as-hell erection split Aidan's crease.

The body on top of him shook, infecting Aidan with need and pain. All of the emotion radiating off Ethan pushed aside the frisson of logic living inside Aidan that said this wasn't right.

Ethan buried his face in the back of Aidan's neck, his words muffled as he spoke. "Let me fuck you, Aidan." He rocked his hips into Aidan's backside and licked a wet strip up the back of Aidan's neck. "I don't know anything else but you right now." He smoothed his hands along the length of Aidan's arms and spread his fingers between the back of Aidan's, linking them as tightly physically as Aidan already felt tied emotionally. Ethan whispered roughly behind Aidan's ear, "Please. I need to be inside."

Oh Christ, I love him so much, and he needs it. Needs me. The clamp of fear dissipated, and the idea of pain or a long, slow, romantic first time no longer mattered. "Lube, baby." Thank God Aidan had been so stupidly optimistic about things working out between them when heading back into town. He reached for his nightstand, stretching his arm. Ethan stayed with him, and his hand remained locked on Aidan's. "I have lube."

Ethan nuzzled his face into the crook of Aidan's shoulder. With a blink of his eyes, a hint of moisture transferred from Ethan to Aidan's flesh. Moving faster, Aidan picked out the soft plastic container from his nightstand drawer.

With frantic movements, Ethan palmed the small tube from Aidan's grasp. In rapid succession, the click of the cap sounded in the dark room, and Ethan spread Aidan's buttocks, exposing his crack to the air. Ethan's fingers, coated in the cool, thick substance, pushed against Aidan's hole with probing insistence. With a burst of force, Ethan pushed his digits inside Aidan's body.

Pain filled Aidan's ass and pulled at his stretched ring, coating a quick layer of sweat over his skin. Before Aidan could process this new level of intimacy, Ethan pulled his fingers out and replaced them with the head of his cock, shoving all the way home on one hard thrust.

Aidan's asshole went up in a flame of fire. "Oohhh shit ... shit…" His entire rectum pulsed with confusion and discomfort at the taking. When Ethan withdrew and sank right back in, stuffing Aidan full with thick, hard cock, Aidan choked and dug his fingers into the sheets. He squeezed his eyes shut in an effort to block away the hurt.

At the same time, Ethan bit Aidan's shoulder, breaking skin. Almost inhuman noises escaped Ethan, and he started a furious, frantic pounding of Aidan's ass. His hips thrust against Aidan's backside again, and again, and again, fucking Aidan with an out-of-control coupling, something that transcended making love or even sex, and changed the act into something Aidan could only feel as the raw mating of one soul that required another to survive. Pure, unfiltered need poured out of Ethan and dripped down onto Aidan, covering him in something primal, which in turn seeped into Aidan and overrode the physical pain.

Only Ethan existed now.

Nothing else mattered.

"Oh yeah…" Aidan bucked his hips back and pushed against the piercing slide of Ethan's cock in his burning channel. "Fuck me, E." He became so aggressive himself it almost felt like he tried to throw Ethan off his back. "Fuck me hard."

Ethan cried out, his voice filling the bedroom with hoarse desperation. He reared up onto his knees, but kept them connected with a bruising hold on Aidan's hips. "Aidan..." Ethan sounded like he barely had a voice anymore. "Please... Aidan." Breathless, he sawed in and out of Aidan's chute with piston-fast strokes. "Need you."

"Yours... Oh!" Aidan gasped, bracing his hands into the bed as he accepted Ethan's fucking. He didn't feel an ounce of physical pleasure from Ethan's cock shafting his ass, but Aidan reveled in the hands holding his hips prisoner, and in the fact that it was Ethan behind him, inside him, finally, after all these years. Swirls of joy coiled inside Aidan over that knowledge, hardening his cock beyond painful. "I belong to you."

Shoving them both back down onto the bed, Ethan covered Aidan and started thrusting into him in a rudimentary, shallow pumping that felt like something they might have done as teenagers. "Mine," he whispered roughly against Aidan's neck. "Mine."

"All yours, Ash." As Aidan said that, the man on top of him stiffened suddenly. "Always," Aidan added, turning the one word into a vow.

Ethan drove his cock home in one brutal thrust. He shuddered, and then scrambled to link his hands in Aidan's within the rumpled sheets. Like a quiet rainstorm after a hurricane, Ethan's cock swelled in Aidan's ass. Liquid heat took over Aidan's sore passage as Ethan dumped hot spurts of cum inside Aidan , each pump of his hips jetting more cum into Aidan's quivering channel, filling him with emotion that right now defied words.

Aidan's ass throbbed with the rough taking, but his stiff dick jutted with ridiculous hardness, needful of relief. His erection sandwiched between the bed and his stomach, Aidan whimpered as his ultra-sensitive length rubbed against the sheets, sending shivers of painful pleasure straight down to his toes. As if that almost-silent noise sent Ethan a telepathic signal, the man pulled out, flipped Aidan over, and swallowed half his cock in one move.

"Ohhhh Christ," Aidan moaned. Wet warmth and suction greeted Aidan's prick, surrounding him in the only bath his cock ever wanted again. Ethan pulled up with a tight drag and then flattened his tongue along the underside as he went back down and gave Aidan a blowjob that defied all of his most explicit fantasies. Aidan reveled at how much of his penis took over Ethan's mouth, and he somehow got even harder watching the O of Ethan's beautiful lips surround him with every up and down suck.

Squirming against the powerful sensations, Aidan struggled not to thrust and take more, but his balls started to squeeze and pull up, signaling his end. A line of tingling raced up and down his spine, and he could not believe it, but his ass channel squeezed with wanting, at the exact same time. "Oh, damn it..." Aidan grabbed one of Ethan's hands and sucked two fingers into his mouth, drenching them in saliva. "Fuck me,

E, fuck me." He drew up one leg and shoved Ethan's hand to his crack, guiding it down until it hit his asshole. "Shove your fingers inside and make me come."

Ethan looked up right then, his blue, blue eyes shining bright in the darkness, and jammed his fingers deep inside Aidan's ass.

Aidan's face pulled taut, and he bared his teeth as everything hit him at once. "Ahh ... ahh..." His chute clamped down and dragged Ethan's fingers even farther inside, naturally taking him to the sweet spot Aidan had only ever wanted this man to know. Ethan impaled Aidan with those two fingers, and with his other hand, he wrapped up the base of Aidan's cock and squeezed.

With the firm rub over his prostate, a tight hand jerking him off, and a pair of lips that put a serious lick on the head of his dick, Aidan bowed off the bed and succumbed to orgasm. Not a damn thing pretty about it, he spurted, his face contorting as he blew his wad, filling Ethan's mouth with seed. Aidan's muscles tightened and released with each jerk of his body, but Ethan stayed right with him and never let go of his cock.

Eventually, Aidan stopped shaking, and he had no more semen to give. His member finally slipped free of Ethan's hold and flopped against his thigh. Ethan stayed right where he was. He closed his eyes and laid his head against Aidan's lower belly. Sliding his hands down the outside of Aidan's legs, Ethan wrapped a tight hold around Aidan's thighs. Everything about the way Ethan looked and held onto Aidan spoke of a scared child clinging to an adult, and Aidan's concerns of before pushed their way back into his thoughts.

He threaded his fingers through Ethan's hair and brushed the blond tufts into a semblance of order. "Ash."

"I know you; I just need to stay with you." Ethan didn't open his eyes, but he clung tighter to Aidan's legs, breaking Aidan's heart. "Let me stay with you." He trembled. "That's all I want."

With a sigh, Aidan left Ethan to his rest. He figured Jayne must have taken a turn for the worse, although with the upbeat person he'd witnessed last night he found that hard to believe. Everything must have caught up to Ethan at once, and guilt stabbed at Aidan for adding to Ethan's upset these last weeks. Maybe he should back off, even more than he already had, and give the man some space to process one upheaval at a time. At the same time, Ethan had come to *him* tonight, instinctively searching out something that his deepest soul considered safe and familiar.

Tonight that was Aidan.

Aidan didn't intend to turn his back on the man he loved.

Running his fingers through Ethan's hair, Aidan did his best to be a safe place for his best friend to lay his head. "All right, baby. Rest and stay as long as you need." Ethan snuggled against him, already fast asleep. Aidan whispered, "Stay forever."

With a hand resting on Ethan's head, a half hour later, Aidan dropped off to sleep.

RIIINNGG. RIIINNNGG. RIINNNGGG.

Aidan rolled over in bed, cursing as the incessant ringing of the alarm clock dragged him away from sleep. He reached out and slapped his hand down on the snooze button, determined to get ten more minutes of rest.

The ringing didn't stop, and that's when the memories of last night -- well, early this morning truthfully -- crashed over him with the power of a tidal wave.

Ethan. Here. Sex.

Aidan rubbed the sleep from his eyes and took in the mess of his bed, where he now lay alone. He crawled out of bed, but his gut twisted, and he knew he would not find Ethan anywhere in this house.

"Shit."

Riinngg. Rinnngg. Riinnggg.

The phone. The obnoxious ringing was the damn landline, which had come with the house. Everything was outdated, and Aidan tended to believe the many comments that nobody had lived in this little house as more than a visitor in over twenty years were true.

Naked, Aidan tread on the cold floor to the living room, hissing at the new soreness in his ass. *Ah, well, it was worth it, to have that short time of closeness with Ethan.* He would take more of the same in a heartbeat, if Ethan were here right now and threw him over the arm of the couch to fuck him again.

Snatching up the phone, Aidan bit off a terse, "Hello. Morgan here."

"Aidan, thank God." He recognized his sister's voice. "I was beginning to think you were never going to pick up. I've called your cell phone at least five times. I figured you'd be out running and then doing errands, but I finally gave up. I'm surprised you're at home."

Aidan circled until he found the clock on the DVD player, and then cursed when he saw the time. Almost noon. *Fuck.* Rubbing his face, he said, "I guess I forgot to set my alarm clock." Instantly, he knew that wasn't true. *Ethan turned it off.* "What's up?" Aidan did a quick mental calculation of the day of the week. "Why aren't you in school?"

"I am. I kept saying I have cramps from my period so I could get out of class and call you. I seriously thought Mr. Driver was going to have someone take me to the emergency room. I swear, guys hear the words, cramps, period, menstruation, and they just freak out."

"Get to the point," Aidan muttered, "or get back to class."

"Right, sorry." A popping sound came through the phone, and Aidan figured his sister was chewing gum. "I wanted to call to say I was sorry about Mrs. Ashworth passing away."

"Wait." No longer tired in the slightest, Aidan's heart seized. "What did you say?"

"It's all around the school," Maddie shared. "Mr. Ashworth -- Ethan, but I have to call him Mr. Ashworth when I'm here -- and his brother took their mother to the hospital last night.

She died early this morning."

Aidan's legs went out from under him and he dropped to the couch.

Oh no. He was so wrecked. I should have guessed. Aidan sat there going over the words Ethan had used last night, tried to process the information, and what had happened because of it. Christ, Jayne had seemed so upbeat last evening. How could things turn so fast?

After a prolonged silence, Maddie spoke, reminding Aidan that he was still on the phone. "You're not saying anything, Aidan. Mrs. Ashworth dying is not even why I called. You didn't know?"

"I didn't." Thickness clogged Aidan's throat and made his voice sound funny. "What did you need? Why did you call?"

"Well, I was getting a drink of water at the fountain that's by the teacher's lounge," Maddie said, on a roll again. "The door was open and I heard the teachers in there talking about Mr. Ashworth. They said he didn't show up for work this morning, no call or anything. Ms. Kelley, she's the assistant principal, she apparently went to the hospital, while Mr. Gordon, the principal, drove out to his house. He's not in either place. Mr. Gordon talked to Wyn and learned that Mr. Ashworth left the hospital right after everything happened, and Wyn hasn't seen Ethan since. Because of how I saw you two talking so intensely last night, I thought you'd want to know." Aidan heard a rustling noise, and then Maddie's voice grew solemn. "Aidan, it looks like Ethan has disappeared."

Chapter Nine

"Damn it, damn it, damn it." Aidan turned in a circle, right in the place he'd stood when he'd kissed Ethan for the first time. On that day, he'd known his heart would be forever tied to this accidental best friend that he'd fallen in love with; he just hadn't known it would take more than a decade for them to be together.

Shadows filled the woods this day, and every time Aidan exhaled, it looked like he blew a puff of smoke. Early spring nights could still get very chilly in the area, and he didn't like not knowing where Ethan would hole up for the cold night ahead.

Aidan held a flashlight in one hand, but shoved the other in his pocket. As he walked back to Ethan's cabin where he'd parked his truck, he waved the light from one side of the makeshift path to the other, hunting for someone hiding in the early patches of darkness. He'd thought for sure he would find Ethan in these woods somewhere; this was where he had come time and again for comfort and to be alone when they were teenagers.

Not this time.

"Where are you, Ash?" Aidan talked to the quickly approaching night, seeking answers from thin air. "You came to me last night. I can help. Why won't you come to me again?" *Wait*. Maybe he had. Maybe Ethan was waiting at Aidan's home right this very minute. Only, here Aidan was, searching the haunts of their youth.

Aidan picked up his pace and then quickly progressed to a full sprint run. He skidded to a halt beside his truck and climbed inside, pausing only long enough to pull his cell phone out of his pocket before revving the engine and heading back to town.

With Dev working a shift at the firehouse, Aidan cursed, but went ahead and dialed his sister's number. He put it on speaker and set the phone in a cubby on the dashboard.

On the third ring, Maddie picked up. "Did you find him yet?" she asked, throwing Aidan for a loop -- for about two seconds. *Of course*. Maddie had witnessed the heated words in front of Ethan's mother's house. She was nearly eighteen and probably knew a little something about relationships and attraction, even if he wished she didn't. It didn't take a genius to put two and two together and come up with a different kind of romance. When she'd called him from school half a dozen hours ago, she'd fully expected him to go out looking for the man. *She knows I'm gay.*

Right now, Aidan didn't have time to care about his sister figuring out that he was in love with Ethan Ashworth. "I haven't found him yet," he finally answered. Navigating the unpaved road with two hands on the wheel, he swore aloud, both for the rough conditions *and* for dragging his sister into his screwed up love life. "I've been away from my house for the better part of the afternoon, though, and I'm still a good ways away from town. Can you run over there and see if Ethan decided to show up? If he's not there right now, can you take a quick walk through the house to see if it looks like someone has been there recently?" Maddie knew Aidan didn't leave his home messy or stuff lying around on furniture, in the kitchen, or even in the bathroom. "Dev's at work, or I'd ask him to do it."

"I'm at work too, you know." Aidan heard a distinct grumbling in that brief sentence from Maddie. "But lucky for you Mr. Corsini thinks of me as a granddaughter. I also happen to like Ethan a lot, and hope he's okay. For those reasons, I'm going to get some time off and go look for Ethan, *not* because I'm a girl, and repairing cars, and thus you view my work as apparently less important than Dev's."

Aidan couldn't believe it, but a rumble of laughter escaped him. "Whatever gets you there, sis." Suddenly, gratitude that he still had a sister who loved him choked Aidan up, and he had to pause. With his choice to move away -- even though at eighteen he hadn't believed he had a choice at all -- he easily could have lost Maddie and Dev anyway. Aidan hadn't seen the truth in that back then; all he'd understood was the panic of knowing for certain that he would *never* have his siblings in his life if he'd brought his feelings for Ethan out of hiding.

Taking a couple of deep breaths to release the tightness in his chest, Aidan let the revelation go, for now. After all, he still had one grief-stricken, stubborn man to find. "Thank you, Maddie," he said, his voice still a little scratchy. "For everything. Let me know what you find."

"You do the same," Maddie replied, and ended the call.

Aidan applied the brakes, and let go of the wheel. He clicked End on his cell, but quickly surfed through the calls he'd taken today, searching for Wyn Ashworth's number. The guy had called down to the station, gotten Dev to give him Aidan's personal number, and had called about his brother, hoping Ethan was with Aidan. After explaining how Ethan had turned up at his house for a while -- minus the part about how they'd had hot, frantic sex -- Aidan had admitted he didn't know where Ethan was either. Together, they'd gathered a few people they knew could be discreet and had split up to look for the man. They both knew Ethan wouldn't hurt himself and that he would be mortified if they set an entire town and police force on the hunt for him. At the same time, they both wanted him found. Sooner, rather than later.

Aidan hadn't talked to Wyn since heading up into the

mountains, and he needed to share and regroup. Wyn must not have located Ethan yet either or he would have called. Just as Aidan found Wyn's number and hit Send, the *beep beep beep* of the pager attached to his belt sounded to life. The high-pitched drone kicked Aidan's adrenaline into the next gear before he even looked at the message window. The little piece of technology only went off for one reason.

Fire.

"Son of a bitch." He yanked the pager off his belt and grabbed the steering wheel, putting the device between his hand and the wheel. Reading the information in the lighted window, he grabbed at the unfamiliar address and plugged it into his GPS system, needing to know where to go once he got down from Ethan's mountain. Even though Aidan wasn't on duty, as chief of this type of station it was his job to show up at the fire, no matter what. He had a second set of turnout gear stored in his truck for situations just like this.

Damn it. An apartment building. The fire code indicated in the alert told Aidan it was bad.

Putting the pedal to the floorboard, Aidan prayed his crew was up to the task and that everyone would get out alive.

———

THE BACK END OF TWILIGHT painted the sky an amazing combination of purples, pinks, and blue. Within Aidan's line of sight, the licking flames of a blazing fire encompassing the top two floors of the apartment complex reached high into the rapidly approaching night, painting an almost grotesquely beautiful picture. A firefighter had to respect the power and art of a fire in order to control and fight it, but not become so mesmerized by it that he or she slipped to the other side of the tempestuous love affair with the beast.

Aidan flashed his badge and got through the police barricade, the crowd half a block away already growing five or six lines deep with gawkers. He pulled the brake on his truck, climbed out, and quickly moving to the rear of his vehicle for his gear, while at the same time assessing his people. While suiting up, he noted that although the fire was a consuming one that would be a substantial loss to ownership, his AC had both trucks in proper position and hoses already attached to hydrants, controlling the damage. Two of the men were in the cherry picker, fighting the blaze as well. It appeared the AC had more than enough crew on hand to do the job, and Aidan couldn't help the swell of pride at his men and woman working like a well-oiled machine. They only needed one person in charge, and right now it looked like Marcus was doing a fine job of handling the load.

AC Marcus Pickens had a booming voice; he shouted to the crew outside the building, and had a walkie-talkie right at his mouth directing men that were out of his vocal range.

Aidan strode to his AC, knowing the man already had a set plan in motion. Just as he was about to ask Marcus where he needed help, Marcus brought a second walkie-talkie up to his ear, cursed up a storm, and then moved it to his mouth.

"What the fuck do you mean there might be a meth lab in the basement! Does the girl say yes or no? Fuck! It doesn't matter!" Aidan's heart started to beat well beyond an adrenaline rush at Marcus's words. He raced to the man's side as Marcus brought the other handheld walkie to his lips. "Interior units one, two and three, vacate the premises. I repeat, all units inside the building, retreat immediately. Possible chemical situation in the basement. Get the fuck out now!"

Aidan didn't take exception to Marcus's words or tone. It could be damned hard to hear while inside a fire, and sometimes a good cursing shout broke through when nothing else did. May not technically be proper procedure, but it happened all the time.

He leaned into Marcus so the man would hear him above the noises of the fire and the crowd. "How many people reported inside? Did we get them all out?"

"Looks good, Chief. Got every area needed covered. More than enough of the crew showed for us to get the job done. Pete and Ashworth are on the sidelines too." *Ethan was here?* Static sounded over one of the devices right then, and Marcus stopped to put one of the walkie-talkies to his mouth. "Repeat, Morgan. Repeat. I did not copy."

"...back ... than ... past us..."

Aidan and Marcus cursed at the in-and-out partial message. Damn ancient equipment. Fuck, his brother did not need to get cocky and hurt himself on his first major fire. At that exact moment, firefighter after firefighter burst out from the front of the building, rushing out of the line of commotion toward Engine 2. Aidan breathed a sigh of relief at the large group -- that is until one of them separated and ran to Marcus and Aidan.

After removing headgear and mask, a sweat-drenched Kara grabbed Marcus's arm. "Sir, someone rushed inside past us. Morgan thought he read Ashworth on the jacket so he and Coop went back inside after him."

No, no, no, no.

"Son of a bitch, no good..." Marcus slammed his fist against the side of Engine 2. "I told him we had the interior and exterior covered, and to touch base with the cops to make sure we had a count on the building correct. Bastard knows better." The walkie-talkie went back to Marcus's mouth. "Morgan! Get your..."

Aidan left Marcus to run the show, as he'd been doing from the moment they got the alarm call. Rather than taking over, Aidan ran toward the front of the building, fuming inside with every pounding step. *Stupid, stupid, stupid bastard.* Disobeying a direct order from the top of the chain-of-command put every damn one of the fellow crew at risk. And when Aidan happened to love two of those people... *No the fuck way.* Aidan's insides heated to hotter than the fire itself with every foot he took that put him closer to Ethan Ashworth.

He wasn't foolish enough to think running into a burning building and creating even more chaos was a smart idea, so he grabbed one of his other men and spun him around, purely in order to stop himself from doing just that. "Matt," he addressed the young guy, "go talk to the AC and tell him I told you to get on the horn and call the chief in Madison." Madison was the nearest town with a fire crew that specialized in handling hazards relating to chemicals. "Alert him that we have a possible meth lab that needs to be contained. Tell him to get his crew down here A.S.A.P."

His dark hair a mess and his face a swirl of sweaty grime, Matt Stone nodded and quickly started to walk backward. "On it, Chief."

Above the din of his men and the crowd, Aidan could barely hear the buzz of Marcus's shouts as he directed the men on the hoses, explaining what they needed to do in order to put out this fire before it consumed even one more floor. Aidan wasn't inclined to believe there really was a drug lab in the basement; his education told him the smell of chemicals would have reached the exterior by now if there were. Or, more likely, already heated the volatile chemicals to the point of blowing the entire building to smithereens. Even so, someone had alerted them to a possible threat, and they had to err on the side of caution.

Aidan made a move toward the building, all the while knowing that stepping inside would lose him all credibility with his people, and possibly his job. For fuck's sake, though, he had his brother, Ethan, and another good man inside that inferno, and he could not sit idle. Damn it, maybe he was not cut out for this job. A real chief would know that he could not go inside. A real chief would be able to control the urge to do that very thing. Meanwhile, Aidan stood here fighting the goddamn strongest *need* in his life to tear inside that building and rescue his people. The need to do *something, anything,* tugged at him harder than the day he had walked away from Ethan at eighteen years old. The consuming desire to rescue his loved ones put Aidan's feet to churning and racing toward the broken-down door.

At the last second, Aidan remembered he still had a sister who needed him too, and pulled up short. Just as he started backing away, a cascade of noise and bodies emerged from the apartment building. Two men held each other upright, while a third, the largest, Coop, held a child-sized body in his arms. Coop rushed past Aidan in the direction of the medical unit. Aidan turned on the other two, the fire inside him returning as the men removed their masks and showed their beloved faces.

"You," he pointed at his brother, who wisely took a wide berth around Aidan, "go to the AC right now and find out where he wants your hands next."

"Aidan," Devlin began, "Ethan heard a kid --"

"No." Aidan whipped his hand up and shut his brother right down. "This is not your brother speaking, this is your chief. The next words I want to hear out of you are 'AC, where do you want me?' " If Aidan had the resources to pull his brother from the job right now, he would do it. "Go. Now."

Devlin clenched his fists, and he opened his mouth too. He clearly thought better of it and strode across the pavement in

Marcus's direction.

Aidan finally let himself lift his attention to Ethan. Seeing the man in the flesh after everything they'd done early this morning, and then spending the day worried sick about him and searching for him, snapped what little patience Aidan had left inside him. Ethan looked him right in the eyes, issuing some sort of belligerent dare.

Aidan moved in close and made eye contact, knowing every bit of the piss-and-vinegar toiling inside him showed right this second. Keeping his voice low out of respect, he uttered, "Get on the fucking truck right now."

"You don't --"

"Trust me," Aidan whispered, his tone lethal, "you don't want to start anything with me right now. *Get in the fucking truck*. Engine 1. I'd better fucking see you in that front seat every time I look up, and you'd better goddamn be in it when it gets back to the firehouse. That is not a request. We are not through with this. Not for one second." Aidan's skin heated unbearably, and his lips thinned down to nothing. He barely moved his mouth while issuing his order, but he could not help the ugliness. It was that, or take Ethan down to the ground and fight him until they were both bloody and bruised. Aidan still hadn't ruled that out as an option. "You need to get away from me, Ethan. Right now."

Ethan bared his teeth right back. They looked like two feral animals. Had anyone around them bothered to look at them rather than the raging fire, they would have witnessed everything Aidan and Ethan felt for each other. Didn't matter one damn bit to Aidan. He didn't much care who saw what lived inside him for this stubborn-as-hell, *hurting* man.

Ethan moved, but he didn't make the wide arc that Devlin had. He walked past Aidan as close in physical contact as he could get without touching, so close their breathing mingled for a moment, and their gazes clashed. Their shared, contained passion crackled the very air around them. Ethan paused right in front of Aidan for the longest drawn-out second, holding him prisoner in every way but with his hands, narrowed his stare, and then moved past to the vehicle.

Aidan watched Ethan climb inside Engine 1. They exchanged one more hard glare before Aidan headed back to Marcus to find out where he could be of use.

He needed to do something with his hands. Quickly.

If he didn't jump into the job, he would turn right back around and strangle the man he loved.

CHAPTER TEN

"I overheard the woman saying there was another kid still in the building!" Ethan's voice rose in volume and strength with each word. "The mom was sleeping! The girl didn't tell the woman she had a friend over because she was afraid she'd get in trouble! What in the hell did you expect me to do!"

"I expect you to follow procedure!" Aidan shouted right back into Ethan's face. Hours had passed since the fire, and they now stood in Aidan's office, each looking like a mess. "You fucking know that you *never* rush into a fire without clearing it with the chief in charge. You put yourself, your fellow firefighters, and even that girl at risk by running into that building the way you did. You get new information about a fire, you take it to the person calling the shots at the scene."

AIDAN AND ETHAN | 153

"There wasn't any time!" Ethan planted his hands on Aidan's desk. He bared his teeth as he leaned in, going nose to nose with his opposition.

"You didn't care if there was time, goddamn you." Punching his fist against the wood, Aidan snapped off each word like an automatic weapon firing in rapid succession. "You took a reckless chance because you're grieving."

Ethan drew up and went very, very still. "Don't you dare bring my mother into this."

Aidan reared back. For just a split second, his mouth hung agape. He closed it fast enough and picked right back up as if there'd never been a pause. "Are you fucking kidding me with that shit? You brought Jayne into this the second you charged into that building against all rules and regulations and you damn well know it. You put not only yourself, but potentially that little girl in harm's way."

"She's alive, and that's all that matters to me."

Sighing, Aidan ran his hands through his hair, putting the thick stuff into total disarray. He flipped open the file on his desk and ran his fingers over the top sheet of paper. Tense silence hung heavy in the air. With his breath held, Ethan watched Aidan's fingers move over his file, and Ethan shivered as if Aidan had actually touched his body. He didn't want it to happen, but even with the crushing weight of loss sitting heavy on his chest, it did.

"What if Devlin and Coop hadn't gone back into the building to give you backup?" Aidan finally asked. "What if you got to where the child was, but you couldn't get to her on your own? Then what would you have done? I'll tell you what." Aidan looked at him with a piercing, uncomfortably scrutinizing stare. "You would have wasted precious time having to wait for your fellow firefighters to come back into the building and help you. Valuable time that very well could have been the difference between that child's life and her death."

Aidan moved out from behind the desk and crossed to a window. He yanked up the blinds, braced his hands on the frame, and stared out into the pitch-dark night. His heavy exhale enveloped the office. The sound pulled Ethan to Aidan, not allowing him to stop until he stood right behind the bigger man. That tall body and strong back beckoned Ethan closer, feeding the ache inside him, one that had lessened for just a brief moment this morning while in Aidan's bed. *While inside Aidan's body.*

Ethan moved to slide his arms around Aidan's waist, to tuck into the comfort that for some reason he could only find with Aidan. As he stepped closer, Aidan broke the silence, his voice now a mere raw scratch.

"What if someone else had already found the girl in their search and you got trapped in that burning building looking for someone who had already been rescued?" Aidan asked, his voice scratchy. "I could have lost you." Aidan's entire upper body heaved with those words. "Maybe you don't give a shit about me, I don't really know anymore. But what about Wyn? Your brother might have had to deal with the loss of his mother and his brother in the same day."

Stiffening just as quickly as he'd almost melted, Ethan backed away. "I know I'm only a volunteer, but I've trained for this job for a long time. I don't ever miss a drill, or a meeting, or a shift, and I've never had to be told what to do twice." He turned and moved to the door with two big strides, suddenly revisiting the urge to hit Aidan just as strongly as the desire to embrace him just a moment ago. With his hand on the handle, prepared to leave, Ethan suddenly stopped.

Staring at Aidan's back, Ethan couldn't look away from the once white T-shirt, now a tie-dye pattern of smoke, grime and sweat, and how it covered Aidan's muscles like a second layer of skin. Ethan ached for closeness with this man, but felt a million miles apart. "No matter what you think," he said softly, "I didn't go into that fire with a death wish, uncaring that my brother would lose me too."

"The problem with that statement, E, is that you didn't go into that fire thinking at all, and I can't have that in my men." Aidan turned from the window, and the life firing in his eyes reared Ethan back against the wall. It felt as if he'd opened a door and walked right into the scorching wall of a backdraft. Hardness etched every line of Aidan's face, making him look at least a decade older than his thirty-one years. "The family of that girl might think you're a hero -- fuck, the whole damn town might consider you a hero."

Suddenly, Aidan stalked Ethan with slow, predatory steps. Ethan's adrenaline started racing faster than when he'd run into the fire earlier today. On instinct, he got the door open and quickly backed into the hallway. Aidan didn't alter his route or pace for once second. "But I know the truth," Aidan finally said, his voice cuttingly soft. "I know your emotions were finally let loose today after pretending they don't exist for far too long, and you were out of control." Aidan's nostrils flared and his breathing seemed to be that of an animal. He looked Ethan up and down, and Ethan felt stripped naked. "Just like you were when you came to me this morning."

Ethan shook his head, his heart racing as he continued to walk backward. "No, not the same."

"Yes," Aidan insisted, "exactly the same. Of course, since then you've exhibited so much erratic behavior I don't know what to think anymore. Disappearing for an entire day without telling a soul where you were, and running into that building when you goddamn know better, I know you do. It makes me wonder if you even realize it was me you fucked this morn --"

Fucker! Ethan raged and threw a punch at Aidan's jaw, shutting his mouth before he could utter another heartless word. The man bowed back under the force of the blow, but didn't flinch or retreat, and that only spurred Ethan on more. "You goddamned fucking bastard." He shook throughout the entire length of his body, and fought the urge to slam another fist into Aidan's face. "You were the only thing my mind, body, and soul recognized this morning, you son of a bitch. I sought you out and found you because of this," he jabbed his fist against his heart, "not this!" He hit his palm against his head.

"And you can fucking stand there reprimanding me, and make jabs about what happened between us -- the only goddamned thing that kept me alive this morning and today -- without so much as flinching? You have become a cold-hearted bastard, Morgan. I can't believe how much time I wasted being in love with you. I can't believe for one second this morning I thought I still was." Ethan's chest squeezed with unbearable pain at yet another loss, but he forced himself to stay upright and not let the upheaval churning inside him show on his face. "I won't make that mistake again. Find someone to take my place on the crew." He took Aidan in one last time, steeling himself to see the rugged handsomeness, feel the pang of attraction ... and then walk away from it. Opening the door to the outside, he uttered roughly, "Goodbye. Write whatever the hell you want in that report, because I won't be back."

"Wait!" Aidan rushed the door, but pulled up short as he remembered that he couldn't leave the station. Marcus's shift had technically ended during the fire, leaving Aidan trapped here for the rest of the night and half of tomorrow. "Damn it!" He punched the wall, satisfaction coursing through him as slices of sharp, tingling pain raced along his fingers and up into his arm. He'd been trying to provoke an emotional reaction out of Ethan with his comment. He wanted the man to at least acknowledge what had happened between them this morning. After all, he had run away without a word, and had not looked at Aidan since with any sense of intimacy, or with an awareness that their relationship had changed.

Christ, at least acknowledge that you fucked me! Aidan had wanted to shout, but refused to show the vulnerability. He had been so stupid to keep quiet about what he really felt. Rubbing his sore jaw, Aidan cursed himself some more. *Well, you got emotion out of him, Morgan, you jackass. And you damn well stomped all over his vulnerable heart while you were at it, and possibly lost him for good.*

Shit, shit, shit, shit, shit. Aidan had never been in a real relationship before and he had no fucking clue what to do in one. Burying his hands in his hair, he turned to go back to his office and think through his next move. As he did, he caught a shadow in the TV area, and found Devlin sitting there in the semi-darkness, clearly having heard every word of the exchange.

Fuck. Aidan didn't need this right now.

And what the hell was his brother still doing at the firehouse anyway?

Rubbing his haggard face, he moved back to his office. "We'll talk later," he called out, knowing his brother would hear him. "When I'm in a better mood."

Devlin's chuckle reached Aidan's ears right before he closed his office door.

Gnashing his teeth, Aidan let the wood rattle with a decided slam.

"So you came back for him," Maddie said, her tone even and unreadable. Aidan sat with her and Devlin at his kitchen table. He held his breath, waiting for a bigger reaction. He'd just spent the better part of an hour explaining everything about why he had left Redemption, as well as and what had brought him back. Again, Maddie said, "You came back for Ethan."

"And for you," Aidan quickly responded. "For both of you." He shifted to include a quiet Devlin too. "But yes, I came back for Ethan," *if I can figure out how to stop being an idiot and get him*, "and hopefully still keep the both of you too."

"Goddamn." Maddie rested her chin in her hand, her gray eyes round and wide. "I can't believe Mom did that to you. She ran her own son out of town. That's cold, and I never would have believed it of her."

"That's the real world, Maddie." Devlin's voice had a cutting edge to it. "People like to talk a big game, but when it actually comes to supporting something that might make you the object of scorn or ridicule, they find they have a lot less tolerance than they thought."

"Whatever her reasons," Aidan said, "it's over now. She thought she was doing the right thing." He held each of their gazes for a drawn-out moment. "I can't see wasting any more time holding onto my anger for someone who isn't here anymore to face it. What's done is done."

"Well, don't worry about Dad," Maddie responded. "I make my own decisions now, and I'm not moving away from my brothers or Redemption, no matter what he says. I almost make enough money to live on my own already, so it's not like he can take financial support away from me and have it matter." Sitting up straight, she jammed her finger into the table, punctuating every word. "I'll file one of those petitions with the court if he tries to take me away. I'll be eighteen well before it's resolved."

"Thank you, sis." Aidan grabbed Maddie's hand before she could bruise her fingertip, and gave her a quick peck on it. The tight knot that had formed in his belly from the moment he'd sat her and Devlin down at his table began to unravel some. "Let's hope it doesn't come to that, but I appreciate you're willing to fight."

"Would have been all those years ago too," she grumbled. "Even if I hadn't known what being gay even meant then. I still missed my big brother, and I was sad as hell when you went away, and then when we had to leave after our little visits."

"Me too." He gave her hand a squeeze. "But they were better than nothing. I didn't want to lose you both forever."

A sharp burst of laughter erupted out of Devlin right then, snapping Aidan and Maddie's attention to him. Devlin covered his mouth but it didn't stop the chuckling. Maddie leaned across the table and smacked him in the arm. Aidan glared, while fighting sickness that roiled inside at his brother's callous laughing. Christ, he didn't want his little brother to think he was a joke, just because he was gay.

Maddie hit Devlin again. He "oofed" before sliding his chair out of her reach. "What? Sorry." Devlin held up his hands as another little bubble of humor escaped him. "It's just funny when you think about it, that's all." Aidan and Maddie opened their mouths, but Devlin shot forward and covered both of them, shutting them up before either could speak. "When you have all of the information, and consider that when it comes right down to it, Mom running you out of town didn't matter at all."

Aidan pushed his brother's hand away, adrenaline suddenly racing, although he didn't know why. "What do you mean by that?"

Devlin released Maddie's mouth and sat back down. "I mean," he looked Aidan right in the eyes, "Ethan is fucking hot. If I were a blind man, and couldn't see how into each other you guys are, I might go after Ethan Ashworth for myself."

Aidan's jaw hit the table. "What?" *No way.*

"You heard me," Devlin said. He slid down in his chair and crossed his arms against his chest. "I'm not out in the open or anything, but from what you just told me, I've already been in one more relationship than you have."

Aidan raised a brow. "So then you're saying you've been in exactly one." His voice could not have been drier.

Deep red slashes suddenly marred Devlin's cheeks. "That's what I'm saying."

Jesus. All that worrying his mother had done, and Devlin turned out to be gay anyway. Oh, the irony.

"Wow," Maddie marveled, a big smile lighting up her face. "And here I was all worried about telling my brothers that I like

162 | CAMERON DANE

girls. Guess I needn't have bothered."

Aidan toppled, and Devlin grabbed him before he fell out of his chair. His head reeling with too much data, coming at him too fast, Aidan grabbed the edge of the table for support. "You're serious?" Stunned didn't even begin to describe his thoughts. How could this be? "You're gay too?"

Maddie's eyes twinkled with shards of silver. "No, I'm not." She giggled, and Aidan slipped back in time to when she was just a little girl. "But wouldn't that have been totally mind-blowing if I was?"

"Mom would have been spinning in her grave," Devlin replied, "that's for sure."

"Hey." Aidan shook his head sharply at Devlin. "Don't talk like that. We don't speak ill of the dead. What's done is done. Let's just hope she can be happy for us now, wherever she is."

"Don't know why she'd be happy for you," Devlin shot back pointedly. "You just lost yourself the guy you supposedly love. I was sitting there, Aidan, and I saw Ethan's face when you made that crack about him not knowing it was you he fu --"

Aidan slammed his hand over Devlin's mouth. "Yes, thank you." His tone was decidedly terse. He slid his focus from Devlin to Maddie, and then back again. *Shut up*, he mouthed. "I was there. I know what I said. You don't need to repeat it."

"Oh, please." Maddie rolled her eyes. "So you had sex with Ethan. Did you think I thought you would only kiss each other or something?"

Aidan growled at the ho-hum tone of Maddie's voice.

"You'd better not already know too much about sex, little sister. Straight or gay. You got me?"

"Yeah, yeah. I'm still a virgin." She just threw the words out there, making both of her brothers flinch. "There isn't any boy in this town I want to have sex with any time soon. Is that what you wanted to hear?"

Right now, Aidan didn't even care if she was feeding him a line. He snorted, wondering if that's how most parents felt too. "Yes. Thank you." He looked up to heaven. "I'm saying a little prayer right now that it's actually true."

"It is," she answered easily. "Now I have one question for you."

"Yeah? What's that?"

"Why aren't you out there getting Ethan back, instead of sitting here talking to us?"

Devlin nodded. "She makes a good point. We can talk any time, but you're losing that man a little bit more with every minute you stay away."

"I-I…" Two faces stared right at Aidan, giving him more open support than he ever could have dreamed. Suddenly he couldn't move, and he didn't know what in the hell to do.

Maddie grabbed him by one arm, and Devlin seized the other. They marched him to his front door, pausing only long enough for Maddie to grab his keys out of a bowl. Walking him to his truck, they put him behind the wheel, strapped him in, and turned the ignition for him.

"Go find him." Maddie pointed in the direction of the

mountains. "Get him back. Now."

Devlin slipped his arm around Maddie and pulled her aside. "The way it always should have been, Aidan." As they back-walked to the front door, he added, "Go make it right, brother. Once and for all."

CHAPTER ELEVEN

"I'm sorry I wigged out on you," Ethan said to his brother for the hundredth time. He had already explained how he'd gotten into his car yesterday morning and just started driving, spent some time on the mountain, and then drove around some more, needing to be alone. Then he'd received the pager message about the fire, and based on where he was, got there as soon as he could. Ethan had tried apologizing and explaining everything to Wyn a good seventy-five times in person this morning, but now, here Wyn was, calling to check in on Ethan, again. "I'm not going to turn off my cell phone and disappear again. I promise."

"You scared the shit out of me, E," Wyn answered, his voice clipped and hard. "So you'll forgive me if I call you hourly just to make sure I can still reach you. I've seen enough accidents in my line of work that I had a hell of a bad visual of what could have happened to you yesterday while you were in such a bad place. It's going to take some time for me to get them out of my head. You're just going to have to fucking deal with the consequences of what you did to me." He paused for a long, drawn-out moment. "Us. What you did to us. You had Aidan going crazy with worry too."

Guilt and anger swirled inside Ethan. The uncomfortable sensations had him pacing the length of his cabin, needing to move. *Aidan.* Pain stabbed Ethan in the chest, as it had done every time he replayed Aidan's cruel taunt in his head. The thought that the man would even consider *for one second* that Ethan didn't care that it was Aidan he had made love to yesterday morning, killed him. God, Ethan had hardly been in a state to have a conversation, but he remembered every goddamned minute he'd spent in Aidan's bed feeling safe, and alive, and connected to this earth because it had been Aidan, and only Aidan, with him.

The reason he had needed Aidan in the first place fought to edge its way into his head and heart, but Ethan dug his fingers into his leg and forced another pain front and center to his mind. *She's in a better place now, man, just remember that. She's in a better place.* Ethan kept breathing and telling himself that mantra, as he'd done all morning at his brother's side while making arrangements for the funeral. Wyn had been an unbendable force, stirring pride in Ethan every step of the way.

Wyn's strength didn't surprise Ethan, after all, his brother was a skilled, trained cop. But having him there today to help handle the well-meaning sympathy proved to Ethan just how tough a young man Wyn had become. Immeasurably so, after the last day and a half when his big brother had temporarily mentally checked out of the game.

"E?" Wyn broke Ethan out of his thoughts, snapping him back into the moment. "Do you need me to come over there? Never mind, you don't get to answer that for the next few weeks. I'm coming over right now. We'll hang out."

"No, no. I'm back to myself now."

"That's what I'm worried about," Wyn replied, his voice harsh. "It's your normal self who hides everything you feel, which is why you were thrown so hard when the doctors told us about Mom."

Growling, Ethan prowled his cabin with his hackles rising on end like a threatened animal. "Stop making me sound like some automaton that doesn't have any emotions."

"I didn't say that." Wyn corrected. "I didn't say you don't have feelings; I said you don't let anyone else see them."

God, Ethan was getting damn sick of listening to people say he didn't express himself. Especially from someone like Wyn, who wasn't exactly a faucet of sharing and tears either. Hearing his brother make the accusation slipped Ethan back to the firehouse and his heated exchange with Aidan. Aidan's taunt, so close to Wyn's just now, had sliced Ethan open and made him *feel* more pain than he ever goddamned wanted to experience again in his life. *No, don't think about that.* He would not give Aidan that kind of power over him again. Fuck, Ethan hadn't meant to give it to him again in the first place. But with everything so raw inside him after his mother had died, he'd had no control in going to Aidan, and even less when seeking that need for connection, acceptance, comfort, from someone who knew his soul inside and out.

Only Aidan knew Ethan that intimately. Thirteen years apart hadn't changed that truth. At least not deep down in that place where the subconscious took over the heart.

"You're scaring me again, man," Wyn said, snapping Ethan out of his wandering thoughts once more. "I'm gonna come over."

"No, don't. You don't need to worry about me. Besides, I talked to Kara a little while ago and she's going to drive out as soon as her shift ends. I won't be alone."

"I can call her and confirm that, you know."

"Go ahead, *Mom*." As soon as Ethan said it, his heart squeezed, constricting a band around his torso. "Sorry." His voice roughened on the apology.

"It's okay," Wyn said, his voice equally textured. "It really was like I was channeling her for a second there. She would have said exactly that."

Guilt at his selfishness rolled through Ethan again. His brother was suffering too. Wyn didn't have anyone special in his life to help him, even so briefly as Aidan had done for Ethan. "How about you, Wyn? Do you need to come over? I don't want you to be alone if you don't want to be. Come and hang with me and Kara."

"Nah, I've got plans." Wyn's thick chuckle came through the phone. "I'm going to check on Aunt Estelle to make sure she's okay at the house with Oz, and then some of the guys are gonna take me out and let me drink until I can't remember anything. They'll make sure I get home okay."

Oz. Ethan's dog seemed to understand what had happened, and had now attached himself to Ethan and Wyn's aunt -- their mother's sister -- just as completely as he had to Jayne. Ozzie was intuitive, and if his big dog heart thought Aunt Estelle needed his company, Ethan would let his dog stay with her for as long as needed.

"Ethan." Wyn broke into his thoughts. "Are you still there?"

"Yeah. Sorry." Ethan shook his head, and traveled back to Wyn's previous comment. "A few drinks with the guys sounds like a good idea." Some of the tightness eased from Ethan's chest. Wyn's cop buddies were good men and wouldn't let him drink beyond a certain limit. "I might have a few myself."

"Don't do it alone," Wyn advised. "That's too sad to think about. At least wait for Kara."

The solid knock of a fist on his door right then got Ethan moving across his cabin.

He shook his head at the timing. "Your wish is my command," he shared with Wyn. "How'd you make that happen? That's her now."

"I'm just that good," Wyn said.

Ethan opened the door. If his brother uttered anything else, it didn't penetrate Ethan's brain.

Aidan, tall and big and looking darkly intense, with a nasty bruise from Ethan's fist coloring his jaw, forced his way inside the cabin, taking over the space.

Oh fuck.

Before Ethan had a chance to form a thought and push him back out, Aidan snaked his hand around Ethan's neck and yanked him close. Aidan's eyes, so piercing, bespoke solitude and desperation with an intensity that grabbed at Ethan's heart.

"What do you want?"

"We talk afterward," Aidan commanded, his voice terribly rough. He planted his palms on Ethan's chest and twisted his fingers in the material of his T-shirt. With such close proximity, their lips nearly grazed against one another, and Ethan's heart raced out of control. Then Aidan went and made it beat a thousand times faster. He plastered himself against Ethan, transferring insane body heat to Ethan's chilled skin, and whispered against his lips, "This time I want you. *I want you.*" He grabbed the phone out of Ethan's hand.

"Wait!"

As Aidan said, "*I want you,*" a third time, he put the phone to his ear. "Whoever you are, he'll call you back." Aidan tossed the phone aside, letting it clatter to the floor without ever looking away from Ethan's face. "We need to get this fixed between us today." He reached down for the zipper on Ethan's jeans. "But right now, I need to be naked with you."

The intensity sank right into Ethan's soul, panicking him. "You…" Damn it, he couldn't think with Aidan standing so close to him. "Me…"

"Us, Ash." Aidan scraped his lips against Ethan's, drawing out a tremble. Pulling back just a sliver, Aidan let blur of their gazes connect, and turned the shiver into a shake. "It has always been us," he said, washing the heat of his words over Ethan's mouth like another caress. "You and me. I don't want anyone else; I never have. Only you." Aidan slid Ethan's zipper down, the noise a soft sigh, as if the two halves of metal teeth were happy to part. "Always you."

The words, the emotion, the sheer need in Aidan, dragged Ethan to a place it terrified him to go. Looking into Aidan's eyes, he knew he must have looked the same way when he'd run to Aidan, desperate for this exact closeness. Seeing it in Aidan now, Ethan finally understood what he had done to Aidan when he'd disappeared without a word, and then when he'd so recklessly ran into that burning building. *He must have felt just like I did when he left me all those years ago.*

"Ash…" The word escaped Aidan as a raw plea.

Oh God; I can see it. The truth sank into Ethan's very pores, invading him as he watched layers of pure emotion play over Aidan's stark, handsome features, witnessing everything the man felt firsthand for the first time since graduation day. *He loves me. Holy shit, he still loves me.*

"Ash," the man in front of Ethan quaked, "please."

Ethan didn't know how in the hell they'd gotten to this

place, or even if it was right, but he suddenly knew he didn't want to be anywhere but in Aidan's embrace.

Slipping his arms around Aidan's waist, for the second time in as many days, Ethan put himself at risk and walked right into a fire. "Fuck me, Aidan." He pulled the big, beautiful man across the room to the bed -- in the cabin he had built for Aidan. Tugging, he tumbled them onto the bed, tangled in each other's legs and arms. He met Aidan's gaze, so beautiful, so open, and so *ready* to be here -- right at home. "Make love to me." He sank his fingers into Aidan's hair and pulled him down until their lips touched. Brushing against them, he finished, "Take me, the way you should have done thirteen years ago."

"Oh shit, baby." Aidan's eyelids fell closed. A wave of overwhelming love washed over him and hit him low in the gut. This was it; the start of everything he'd always wanted. A life with Ethan Ashworth. Christ, he could not screw it up.

Ethan shifted under him just then, grazing their jean-covered cocks against one another. Opening his eyes, Aidan hissed and pushed against Ethan's crotch, needing a firmer touch. Hard ridges ground against one another, but it simply wasn't enough. He needed Ethan.

All of him.

"Clothes." Aidan reared up in a straddle position and ripped off his heavy shirt, uncaring if he damaged it beyond repair. "Too many clothes." He drew his T-shirt over his head and tossed it aside too, where it floated to rest over the foot of the bed. Then he went right for the snap on his jeans.

Ethan beat him to the zipper, pushing Aidan's fingers aside. "Let me." Their gazes found each other's, and Aidan's chest heaved raggedly with the connection. He felt the tug to get closer and swore this was the most intimate moment of his life.

"I love you." The words rushed out of Aidan, scraping his throat bare. "I think I have from the moment you came to my rescue in that parking lot. I never knew I was gay until I saw you. You made my cock ache that very night. I got under my covers and jerked off while thinking about you." Aidan's breath caught as Ethan pushed his hands inside Aidan's jeans. Ethan eased the fabric down past Aidan's hips, springing his cock free. Aidan confessed, "I've jerked off a million times more since we've been apart while dreaming of you."

"Me too." Ethan lifted up, pressed a kiss against the flat of Aidan's belly, and then licked with the wonderful heat of his tongue. As Ethan looked up, their gazes caught. He worked his shirt off, losing the stare when the fabric briefly covered his face and head. As soon as the shirt hit the floor, they found each other again. Aidan got lost in a lake of Caribbean blue, his favorite color in the world.

"Don't run from me again." Ethan's chin stayed strong, but his voice wavered. "I couldn't survive it."

The small tremor gutted Aidan right up the middle. "Never again, Ash." He made those words a solemn promise, not only to Ethan, but also for himself. Leaning into Ethan, he lowered them both to the bed and settled their mouths against one another. "I'm not ever leaving Redemption without you at my side." He flicked the tip of his tongue against the seam of Ethan's lips, seeking entry, and thought he reached heaven when Ethan opened up and let him inside.

Moaning, Aidan sank in, meeting the slide of Ethan's tongue in a languid tangle of hot, wet need. Quickly it was not enough, so he dug his fingers into Ethan's jaw and forced the man to open wider, desperate to get in deeper, while fighting the desire to devour Ethan one piece at a time. He pushed his other hand in between their bodies and fumbled with Ethan's jeans and underwear, awkward in his effort to get them at least down to his thighs. Christ, he wanted his hands, his mouth, his cock … hell, everything, on Ethan's straining erection.

"Here, here." Ethan broke the kiss, panting heavily against Aidan's mouth. "Let me help you." He shoved his hands down too. Together, they toed off shoes and socks, and struggled out of jeans and underwear as well, all while continuing to bite and nip at each other's lips.

With the last pieces of clothing removed, nothing but the smooth, pure heat and muscle of Ethan's fit, gorgeous body rubbed against Aidan, stealing his very breath away. The man's inner thighs grazed the outer line of Aidan's. His hard stomach and chest pressed into Aidan too, and the sinewy steel of his arms held Aidan in a firm hold, sending Aidan's desire for Ethan into overload. It was all too much to feel at once. Aidan suddenly strong-armed into a pushup stance so he could get a visual of everything that felt so damn *good.*

Afternoon sunshine streamed in through the picture window, sending streaks of pure light over Ethan's body, haloing his blond hair and highlighting his perfectly honed muscles. *Good Christ, no one person should be this beautiful.*

Ethan rolled over then and gave Aidan a second picture of perfection. "I have stuff," Ethan said, but Aidan barely processed the information. Aidan stared, his mouth dry, at the stunning lines of Ethan's broad, golden-tan back and the inverted dip of his spine that arrowed a line right to a smooth, tight ass. Jesus, Aidan wanted to hold Ethan open and lick down the crack, tasting everything Ethan had to offer before plugging him deep with the hard length of his cock. Aidan lifted his hand, his fingers itching to feel the texture of flesh, but Ethan shifted and pushed back under Aidan again, taking away the sight.

Ethan looked up, his eyes unfathomably wide. "This is it." He curled his hand around a bottle of lubricant, but quickly buried it and his fingers in the rumpled, twisted-up comforter. "It's all I have. There's no... I'm okay. I know I didn't use one when I came to you... I shouldn't have done it like I did yesterday morning, but..."

Aidan covered Ethan's mouth, effectively shutting him up. "I'm okay too. I trust you. I didn't want a condom between us yesterday, and I don't want one now."

Ethan pried Aidan's hand off his lips and slid it down his body, holding it at his stomach. "I don't want one either. Make love to me, Aidan. Touch me," he left Aidan's hand on his abdomen and glided his fingers up Aidan's arms to his shoulders, "and make me forget everything but you."

"Damn it, Ash." The emotional ramifications of being naked in bed with this man, with both of them purely in the moment, slammed through Aidan, choking his words. "I want you so damn much. I don't know where to begin."

"Wherever you want." Ethan touched Aidan's lips, pulling on the lower one with the pad of his finger. "We have forever to get to it all." Ethan's eyes, finally shining so openly with desire, worked as a riptide and pulled Aidan under the water.

Groaning, Aidan dropped back down and delivered a fast, savage kiss, sweeping Ethan's mouth with deep forays, where every taste he took fed his ache for more. Tearing his mouth away, he ran the flat of his tongue along Ethan's jaw line to his ear, sending shivers of awareness to every nerve ending that scraped across the light stubble. "I have to learn your body." He swirled around the earlobe and dipped inside with a quick flick. "I want to lick every damn inch of you."

"Ohhh fuck…" Ethan grabbed onto Aidan's upper arms and squeezed with a death grip. "Please do." He lifted his hips into Aidan, smashing their cocks together. "Whenever, however you want."

Aidan smiled against the crook of Ethan's shoulder and then kissed the sensitive patch of skin. Almost purring, he said, "Feels like I know which place you want me to learn first." He curled his hand around Ethan's hard cock and stroked up and down its thick length, following the line of raised vein on the underside with his finger. Damn, Ethan's heat felt perfect against Aidan's palm. "Liked what I did down there the first time, did you?" His taste buds tickled to life, reliving the bitter saltiness of Ethan's cum spurting in his mouth. *Mmmm.* "Want me to do it again?"

"Fucking A, Morgan," Ethan growled. He squirmed under Aidan, pushing his rigid length in and out of the circle of Aidan's hold. "I'll goddamn hurt you if you don't."

Every time Ethan spoke, Aidan couldn't keep a grin off his face. "All in good time, baby." He began his journey down Ethan's incredible chest. "All in good time." So much rock-hard muscle under his lips, all with the hint of perspiration, teased Aidan's senses and sank into his blood.

Aidan reluctantly released Ethan's penis. He ran his hands up Ethan's sides to his armpits, pushing until he had Ethan's arm stretched high above his head. Ethan's entire upper body flexed and shifted to accommodate the move, but he also adjusted and spread his legs wider, letting out a soft noise that gave away how much he liked it. Aidan loved the picture Ethan made, no matter the position. He settled in between those spread thighs, kissed his way to a big, flat nipple, and latched right on.

With the first pulling suck, Ethan arched his back right off the bed. "Oh God, Aidan … Aidan…" He clamped his thighs on Aidan's hips, but he didn't move his arms. Instead, he dug into the bed sheets and bunched them in his hands, holding on tight. "Don't stop." The tiny pinpoint of his nipple twisted and grew pebble-hard against Aidan's tongue, responding to the licks and nibbles. Aidan's dick twitched with need. He pushed it into the covers to relieve the clawing desire for a touch, but otherwise ignored his cock. He intended to savor every second Ethan gave him and prove they were meant to be together in every way.

He sucked on Ethan's nipple, and then opened his mouth wider against Ethan's chest and sank his teeth in, leaving a mark he damn well knew would show tomorrow. Possession hummed through Aidan, and he kissed his way across the plane of Ethan's torso to do the exact same thing on the other side. Ethan jerked beneath him at the bite, but he dug his heels into the bed and pumped his hips up into Aidan at the same time, rubbing his erection into Aidan's stomach with a hard grind.

Aidan bit again, and Ethan whimpered, "So good." With his hands anchored in the bedding above him, Ethan writhed his entire body along the length of Aidan's. In the process, he strung every nerve ending in Aidan's body tighter than an archer's bow. "You feel so fucking good."

"Need you, Ash." Aidan buried his face in Ethan's flesh and then licked a line down to his navel, shielding himself as he shared a piece of his life and soul ... if Ethan listened closely to the words. "Doesn't work unless it's you." Before he could blurt out anything else, Aidan dipped lower and forced half of Ethan's cock into his mouth.

Ethan cried out and speared up, jamming more length past Aidan's lips, pushing nearly to Aidan's throat.

Aidan grabbed the base of Ethan's penis and started working

it in the tight glove of his fist, loving that the burn pulsing inside almost set his hand on fire. Velvet-heat and saltiness filled Aidan's mouth with everything *Ethan*, blossoming his almost-virgin taste buds to crackling with joy, almost like Pop Rocks used to do for him as a kid. Groaning, aching, Aidan sucked hard, without finesse, just eager to get any part of Ethan as near to him, close to him, *inside* him, as he could. He reached between Ethan's legs and cupped his balls in hand, marveling at the smooth texture of the skin, so different from the light fur that covered his own. The weight sat big and heavy, full of cum, drawing more excitement out of Aidan as his mind spun crazily with the many ways he could draw all that seed out of his man. He massaged Ethan's sac and gave it a little tug. At the same time, he pulled up on Ethan's prick, letting the length slip from his lips with a little *pop*. All slick and wet with saliva, Aidan wrapped his hand around Ethan's cock and pumped up and down his engorged length, knowing how much his own cock enjoyed a damn firm handjob.

"Umm, yeah … harder." Ethan undulated his hips in time with Aidan's motion, gasping as Aidan accommodated his wish and wrapped his fingers even tighter around Ethan's cock. "Fuck, man, you have nice hands."

Aidan looked up into Ethan's eyes. "You have an even nicer cock."

Ethan's chuckle turned into a groan, and both their focuses dropped back to Aidan's hand around Ethan's dick. Right then, a drop of precum pearled from the long, angry looking slit, growing ever bigger as Ethan moaned and bucked under Aidan's novice touch. The liquid sat there, so tempting, just a hint of the flood this man would give Aidan in a moment, beckoning him for a little taste. Unable to deny himself, Aidan guided Ethan's cock to his lips and swiped the deep slit with the tip of his tongue, murmuring his joy at the small gift. The less intense flavor spread through Aidan, tagging him on the inside where he could never get free of the brand.

Thank God, he never wanted to get away.

Another bead, more proof of Ethan's equal desire, formed. Aidan kissed the head of Ethan's prick and rubbed it over his lips, transferring the sheen of pre-ejaculate from Ethan's cock to Aidan's mouth. Licking it away and swallowing down the small hint of what was to come, Aidan dipped down for more, sipping from Ethan's opening, pulling every piece of Ethan out that he could get and taking it for himself.

"Too much." Ethan hissed, drawing Aidan's focus up to his face. "You'll make me come."

"Want you to," Aidan confessed, keeping their stare locked as he went back down on Ethan's rearing erection.

Ethan looked down the length of his body, his eyes a smudged blue, hazy as he stared at Aidan's mouth working his cock. Aidan couldn't stop. He laved his tongue all over Ethan's jutting pole, licking every place where he didn't use his hand to jerk him into a frenzy. Aidan tried to give Ethan a little bit of everything, but Aidan couldn't help it, he went right back to his main source of pleasure, again and again. He needed a mouth full of Ethan's thick penis. Aidan spread his lips wide and bobbed down the burning length again, giving his lover the blowjob he'd delivered in his mind a million times.

Over the years, Aidan had dreamed of touching Ethan all over and doing a thousand different things to the man's body, all of them intimate, some of them raw and base. Aidan's most fevered dreams had always returned him to his knees, where he sucked Ethan off until the man couldn't take the pleasure anymore and came in Aidan's mouth. Every time Aidan let himself sink into the joy of that particular fantasy, he realized just how much he loved the idea of having a hot cock pulsing in his mouth. When, in all those years apart, Aidan had found many men physically attractive but had never developed feelings for any one of them, he realized that he didn't want to suck cock so much as he wanted to torment, tease, and satisfy *Ethan's* cock.

No one else.

Forcing his throat muscles to relax, Aidan moved his hand away from the base of Ethan's dick. He went down on Ethan, and this time, when he got as far as he thought he could go, he pushed it a little farther.

"Oh fuck." Ethan jerked beneath him. "Too good, too much. Aidan, baby, wait, wait…" In a rush, Ethan let go of the sheets and pushed Aidan's mouth away. "Stop." Reaching between his legs, he grabbed his balls, cursing as he tugged them away from his body.

Hurt stabbed at Aidan. Just as quickly as the sharp pain hit him, Ethan slipped his free hand under Aidan's chin and drew his face up. Pools of blue looked at him, catching Aidan hard in the heart.

"It's okay," Ethan said. "It's not that I didn't like it." His face heated on a groan. "I liked it too much. I don't want to come in your mouth this time." Ethan soothed Aidan's unspoken fears, as he had always been able to do. "I want to be hard when you fuck me." He let go of his balls and fumbled around in the comforter. "Fuck me, Aidan. Please." He handed over the lube. "Do it now."

Aidan verbally protested the loss, but his dick raged with need, pushing hard against his stomach after being denied for too long. "I want to see you." With hands shaking, he slid them up the underside of Ethan's thighs and pushed his legs to either side of his chest, tilting Ethan's ass into view. "Wanna look at where I want to go." Another one of his most fevered dreams coming true, Aidan used the heels of his hands to press Ethan's ass cheeks wide apart, exposing his tight ring.

Tiny and dusty-rose in color, the starburst striations of Ethan's asshole made Aidan's breath catch. His cock then quickly reared, and his heart raced with need. "Oh Christ," reverence sounded in his voice, "how I want your hole."

"I'm quivering for you inside." Ethan's revelation forced Aidan to look up to his face. Confirming his words with a nod, Ethan added, "Take me. I'm aching for you." He licked two fingers and rubbed over his exposed asshole, eliciting a shiver out of both of them. "Make me yours."

Grabbing up the lube, Aidan knocked Ethan's hand away. He squirted out a good dollop and rubbed it all over his cock. Hissing at the pleasure, he stared at Ethan and fitted the head of his cock to Ethan's snapped-shut hole. "You always were mine," Aidan said, "even when we were apart."

The blue in Ethan's eyes shifted to the colors of the deepest recesses of the ocean. He bumped up against the tip of Aidan's cock, pressing it to his entrance. He did it again, sending the nerve-endings at the top of Aidan's penis into a frenzy.

On the third time, Aidan bore down when Ethan thrust up. Their gazes connected, and Ethan whispered, "I know."

Ethan's confession ripped through Aidan with the sweetest kind of pain. The sentiment grabbed him in the heart, and he shoved hard with all of his weight against the barrier of Ethan's ring. He suddenly broke through to the other side, and rammed his cock home.

"Ohhh fuck…" Ethan grunted and bucked at the taking, but quickly dropped his legs and locked them around Aidan's waist, holding on for dear life. "More … you … deeper."

"Ash…" Gasping through the sharp pleasure that quickly spread throughout his entire body, Aidan pulled out of Ethan's snug channel and thrust again, unable to hold still. The tightest, hottest, most wonderfully suffocating sensation surrounded his cock in a clamping hold, and Aidan had no power to control his need to move, to take more, to slow down, or even to stop. Everything that was Ethan consumed Aidan: his smell, his size, his heat, the burning hold of his ass. As Aidan looked up and met Ethan's gaze, he realized it was the brightness of love shining in the man's eyes that did him in above all the rest.

Aidan dropped down and smashed his mouth on Ethan's. He forced his way inside, taking his man in another way. Ethan kissed him back equally hard, thrusting his tongue into Aidan's mouth and dueling with him. Their kiss was aggressive in every way. Teeth scraped and bit, fingers dug into muscles and hair, and Aidan knew that neither one of them would come out of this encounter unscathed. Aidan didn't want to. He wanted Ethan all over him in visible, physical ways that would show the world what they meant to each other, finally, after all this time.

"So good." Aidan drew upright and held Ethan's legs with a bruising grip, fucking him with relentless, deep strokes. He watched his cock slide inside Ethan's body over and over again, claiming him, and prayed that more than physical passion had gotten the better of Ethan, and that Ethan felt the same. The thought that Ethan might turn away again after they had sex fueled Aidan's insecurity. With a hoarse cry, he increased his pace, sawing his cock in and out of Ethan's passage, forcing him to feel their connection in every way. "Mine." Aidan didn't know if that one word was a plea for an agreement or a statement of fact, but it reached such a needy place inside him that he uttered, "Mine," again, and plowed Ethan's chute to its deepest recesses to deliver his point.

"Yours, Aidan." Ethan twisted and pushed up into Aidan's fucking, groaning and gritting his teeth with every thrust. He looked up, found Aidan's stare, and didn't look away. Ethan grabbed tight onto Aidan's forearms and pulled himself up until their foreheads touched. Looking right into Aidan's eyes, right into his heart, Ethan whispered, "Always yours."

No time to give warning, or even feel it coming on, Aidan crushed his mouth to Ethan's, crying out as orgasm overtook him. "Ahhh, yeeess…" He jerked and swelled, tucked within the scorching tight confines of Ethan's dark tunnel. His lips parted, and he keened with the first jet of seed he shot into Ethan's ass.

Ethan's mouth dropped open too, and their hot breath mingled as one. "Feel you." A sense of shock and wonder filled his voice. "Oh God, I feel you coming inside me."

Aidan reacted on Ethan's response alone and spurted a second wave of release, filling Ethan's channel with hot cum.

Ethan held onto Aidan's shoulders. His head fell back, his eyelids dropped closed, and his ass squeezed down all around Aidan's cock. "Too much … good … so fucking good."

Ethan's spike-stiff erection rammed into Aidan's belly. In a flash, Aidan reached down and took hold of it. Pre-ejaculate streamed down from the slit, slicking the length for a hard pull. "Don't hold back, Ash." Aidan jerked Ethan off with fast, tight strokes, trying with everything in him to give Ethan the feeling of being inside Aidan's ass. "Come all over me and give me everything you've got."

Ethan whimpered. He braced his hands on the bed and put his hips in a furious motion against the circle of Aidan's hand. "Harder." He shoved his cock through Aidan's fist with piston-fast thrusts. "More." Aidan capped the opening of his hand, and when Ethan pushed through this time, his cockhead jammed into a stopping point, an immovable force, and it flung him right over the edge.

"Ohhh ... ohhh ... fuck!" Aidan pulled his hand away just as Ethan let loose and spewed. His entire body shaking, Ethan came in one long orgasm, spraying an arc of milky cum high into the air, where it eventually fell in a hot splash on Aidan's chest and stomach, with some fanning back onto Ethan's belly, pubes and cock too.

His chest rising and falling heavily, Ethan dropped back on the bed and threw his arm against his forehead. Aidan's cock slipped free of Ethan's ass, bringing about one last shiver of pleasure.

It also brought on a giant case of nerves.

There was no turning back now.

"Ethan." Aidan drew the man's arm away from his face, crawled on top of him, and looked into his eyes. Fear of "morning after" regret shook through Aidan, but he would face Ethan once and for all and hold nothing back. "It's time to talk."

Ethan opened his mouth, but right then his front door opened, and Kara called out, "I'm here, sweetie. Tell me what you need me to do."

Aidan's heart fell right into his stomach, and he thought he might be sick.

CHAPTER TWELVE

"Ethan, are you okay... Oh, well..." Kara's voice trailed off as it drifted across the cabin to the bed.

Oh shit. Ethan quickly threw covers over himself and Aidan. *I forgot about Kara.*

Aidan lay on top of Ethan as still as a statue, horror darkening and mapping every line of his face. Ethan could feel the man's heart racing, stamping a frantic beat through his chest and sinking into Ethan's flesh. Aidan's pale eyes turned mossy and then he squeezed them closed. He looked like a kid caught snooping somewhere he wasn't supposed to be, yet he hoped that if he just stood still enough, for long enough, he would be overlooked and not get into trouble.

Ethan couldn't help it, he burst into laughter.

Aidan's eyes popped open and he drilled Ethan with a fierce glare. "Don't laugh."

Right then, Kara said, "Well, crap. Looks like you've worked everything out and I have to find myself a new beard."

Aidan shot off Ethan and spun to face Kara, his mouth hanging agape. "Wh-what?" He glanced down, saw his nakedness, and grabbed the comforter to pull over his lap. As he frantically wiped semen from his chest and stomach, he looked from Ethan to Kara, and back to Ethan. "What did she say?"

Ethan raised a brow. "I told you not to assume you knew anything about my relationship with Kara, but you didn't listen."

Aidan's cheeks turned ruddy, his eyes darkened, and his mouth thinned to a narrow line. Worried about the fast change in his lover, Ethan lunged for Aidan, but the man executed a fast tuck-roll off the bed and moved out of reach. Aidan gathered the comforter around his waist and backed up even farther, not stopping until his legs hit the long banquette bench in front of the picture window.

"Come on, Aidan," Ethan cajoled. "Don't be upset. I was under no obligation to tell you anything. In case you've forgotten, I was damn angry with you when you showed up in Redemption unannounced. Why would I have just come out and told you that Kara and I are just friends?"

"Good friends," Kara added from where she still stood at the door.

"But not lovers," Ethan said.

If anything, Aidan just got even more tense. "I'm starting to feel like a fool here." He curled his hands around the edge of the brick-red cushion and crushed it in his hold. He looked at Ethan, and his eyes blazed. "When I found out you had a girlfriend, I hated like hell thinking my efforts to get you back were going to hurt this woman. Now I'm seeing it's just a big joke between you two." He flicked a glance Kara's way, but quickly came back to Ethan. "Someone needs to start saying more than a cryptic phrase or two, and doing it damn quick."

"I really shouldn't be a part of this," Kara announced. "It's better that you two hash this out without me. I have food from some of the nurses at work." As she walked to the kitchen, she held up two plastic bags. "I'm just going to throw them in the fridge really quickly so that nothing spoils."

"Thanks, sweetie," Ethan said, his heart weighing down with loss again. "Make sure to remember names so Wyn and I can send thank you notes."

Closing the refrigerator, she winked at him as she moved to the bed. "Already taped to the containers." She leaned in and pressed a kiss to the top of his head. "I'll see you tomorrow morning."

The funeral. God, Ethan didn't want to face that yet. "Okay. Thanks."

"And you…" Kara pointed at Aidan rather than backing toward the still-open front door. "The only reason I'm leaving him in your care is because I know you're *him*. You're the up-until-now nameless guy that owned his heart. I suspected it the first time I saw the two of you at the firehouse together, and I knew it for sure when you faced off in front of my house. I can see in your eyes that you love him, Aidan, and I'm damned appreciative that you reamed him a new asshole for running into that building against the rules. That shows me how much you really care. Don't blow it this time, and I don't mean his cock. Take care of him. You got me?"

"I got you." The ruddiness in Aidan's cheeks softened to a rosy blush. "I'm home now, and I'm not leaving him again."

"That's what I wanted to hear." She turned to back up, and her hair swung over her shoulder in a shiny auburn waterfall. "I'll lock the door on my way out." She whipped around one last time and wiggled her fingers at them. "Bye." Both men stared as she breezed out of the cabin in just as big a whirlwind as she'd breezed in.

"Ah Christ." Aidan rubbed his face and leaned back against the window. "This is getting complicated, and I know you don't need complicated right now."

Ethan's chest swelled, filling up with renewed love for this man. He went to Aidan, kneeled in front of him, and took his hands in a loose hold. "It's not complicated, Aidan. I just didn't give you full disclosure before now. I was hurt and angry, and we had a ton of unresolved stuff between us."

"I know, I know." Aidan growled and banged his head against the window. "I can never apologize enough for leaving you without saying a word. I should have believed in myself and been stronger, and I should have had faith that you could help me figure out a way to keep both you *and* my brother and sister, rather than automatically agreeing to what my mother wanted and going away. I shouldn't have been so scared to come back after I realized I would never stop loving you. I should have been braver and faced your wrath long ago instead of waiting for the excuse of a new job before showing my face in Redemption again." Aidan hit his head against the window again, and punched the seat with a furious curse. "I fucking should have been a man and done so many things differently."

"Hey, stop that." Ethan grabbed Aidan, forcing his head out of hitting distance of the window. He curled his hand around Aidan's neck and pulled him forward until their faces nearly touched. "The fact is, if I hadn't been so afraid of hearing you reject me in person, I could have figured out a way to find you and get my answers. Fear held me back just as strongly as it did you. We were kids."

Holding the other man's gaze, seeing true regret in his eyes, Ethan released the past. "I forgot how young we were as I grew older. Each year that went by, where I learned how to make decisions and be an adult, I put more and more of those capabilities on the eighteen-year-old you were when you left, even though realistically you didn't have the coping skills of an adult back then. By the time you showed up here a month ago I was spoiling for a fight and wanting to hear rational reasons and explanations for your choice. I wanted one that a thirty-one-year-old adult would make, not the young man you were back then. With my head in that place, there wasn't any explanation you could have given me that would have been good enough to satisfy thirteen years of questions."

Aidan clutched Ethan's face in his hands, bruisingly hard, and stared into Ethan's eyes. "I'm sorry I hurt you." His voice, so rough, scraped across Ethan like a desperate kiss. "So, so sorry. I missed you, and I wanted you every minute I was away. That never changed." He finally gave Ethan that kiss, clinging, searching, tasting … and full of pain and sorrow. "Please say you believe me."

"I do. I do." Absorbing the pure emotion emanating from Aidan in a blanketing balm, Ethan brushed his mouth against the beautiful hardness of Aidan's. He then grazed their jaws, cheeks, and foreheads over one another's, almost like two newly acquainted animals feeling each other out for trust. As Ethan did, his heart found the answer, and it was: *yes, he's the right one. I'm supposed to be here with him.*

He knew whom he had to thank for helping him see the light.

"The one beacon in my mom's passing," Ethan had to stop for a minute and wait for tightness in his throat to ease up, "is that I went to you because my soul knew, when I couldn't yet face it, that I needed you. Only you. That started the chain of events that brought us back together."

"I'm so sorry, baby." Aidan's eyes shone bright with moisture. "I know how much you loved her."

"I did. We did. Wyn too," Ethan corrected. He paused and

took a deep breath, stabilizing the swirl of loss that struggled to get free. "But I think it was hurting her too much to go on. I think she was ready to leave us a while ago. She just needed to know we would be okay when she went away."

"Did your mother know about us, Ash?" Aidan asked. "When I went to visit her, I don't know, it was as if she could see inside me and knew how I felt about you. It was like she was trying to tell me not to give up. She kept talking about forgiveness, and how true friends can come together again, through anything."

"I never told her." Ethan sat still for a minute and tried to see the past with fresh eyes. "She knew how withdrawn I became after you went away. I'm sure she could see how hurt and confused I was, even though I refused to talk about it. I think she knew what I had with Kara wasn't some grand passion either, even though we were together for five years." He shrugged. "It might not have been much of a stretch for her to guess. Back in high school, she did see us together whenever you came to the house with me. I stared at you an awful lot."

Aidan smiled wryly. "I stared at you just as much."

Heat stole over Ethan's face, and he felt a bit like that sixteen-year-old kid again discovering his first -- his only -- true crush. "Anyone who was looking probably could have guessed fairly easily that I liked you more than most boys like their best friend." Ethan's knees started to ache against the hardwood flooring, so he shifted, his joints popping as he pushed up and sat down next to Aidan. "She was an insightful person, so she probably had a pretty good hunch."

Aidan leaned his head against Ethan's shoulder, making Ethan's heart flutter. "Yeah, I think she did. More than that, I think she was okay with it too."

"She would have been." Now that they were alone again, Ethan pushed the comforter off Aidan's lap, letting it land in a heap on the floor. He took Aidan's big hand in his and linked their fingers, staring at the connection. "Mom would always preach to me and Wyn that we should be honest-to-God, flat-out, madly in love with the person we chose to spend our life with, and that we should be certain they felt the same. She would always say 'that's the only thing I require of your future spouse.' " He smiled. "That's probably why she liked Kara really well, but never asked me when I might get married. She knew Kara wasn't the one."

"And what about Kara?" Aidan shifted on the cushion, drawing a knee up as he faced Ethan. "Who is she, really? Other than someone who obviously took good care of you, and so I'll be forever grateful to her for that."

Ethan smiled, thinking about the tall beauty. "Kara's the best. She is the sister of one of my college roommates. I've known her for a lot of years."

"Where'd you end up going to college?" Aidan's face hardened once again. "There's so much I don't know about you that I should. I've missed so much important stuff in your life."

The rough lines bracketing Aidan's mouth beckoned Ethan, and he tried to soothe them away with his touch. "We'll get it back, a little at a time." He leaned in and pecked a kiss on Aidan's lips, lingering until he felt the man release the tension inside him and kiss Ethan back. Satisfied for now, Ethan pulled back. "I started out here at the community college, which is where I stayed until Mom's first bout with cancer went into remission. After that I transferred to U Maine. I got my Masters there."

"Wow. You worked really hard. I'm proud of you." Aidan chewed on the edge of his lip. "I didn't go to college. I was either training to be or have been a firefighter, from pretty much the day I left Redemption."

"There's no shame in that. It's a noble career, and it's honest work." Ethan looked at Aidan right now, stunningly gorgeous in his nakedness, but went back over the last few weeks and pictured him during any one of their training drills. "Besides, you look sexy as hell in your turnout gear."

"Thanks." They made eye contact, and the sparks of their new sexual relationship arced between them. "So do you."

"Thanks."

Aidan put his hand on Ethan's knee and then slid it up his thigh, making Ethan shiver. Ethan's cock stirred and his skin started to tighten and heat. Aidan leaned in, his stare intent on Ethan's mouth. They both licked their lips, but abruptly, Aidan jerked back. "I'm sorry." He whipped his hand off Ethan's thigh too. "I interrupted and distracted us. You were telling me about how you came to have this relationship with Kara." He wrapped his arms around his drawn knees and locked his hands together, as if he needed to do it so that he didn't reach out and touch Ethan again. "I really do want to know. You said you knew her through a roommate. What else?"

Ethan's dick protested the withdrawal, but he understood Aidan's desire for answers. Ethan still had a bunch of questions himself. They had been apart for thirteen years, and it would take time to fill in the blanks.

"Kara was open and out in college, and dating an older woman she really loved. They were together for a long time. Then one day the woman dumps her out of the blue, saying she was not in love with her anymore. It tore Kara apart."

"Ouch." Aidan winced.

"Yeah." Ethan tensed up for a second, reliving the pain of rejection. He reminded himself that it wasn't true, Aidan hadn't rejected him all those years ago. Ethan's shoulders eased, but he knew it would take time for gut reactions like that to change, now that he had new information. Shaking it off, Ethan went on. "Kara needed a change, and when I told her I'd heard something about a bunch of new positions opening up at the hospital in town she jumped at the chance to move someplace new. I was the only person she knew when she came to Redemption, so we hung out a lot. People started assuming we were dating, and we just sort of fell into letting people believe it. She's a knockout, and she'd have guys hitting on her left and right if she didn't have a boyfriend. At the time, she really wasn't up to fending men off or being the token lesbian on the hospital staff. I wasn't dating anyone, and it was kind of nice when people stopped asking me if there was anybody special after they started seeing me hanging out with Kara. When they found out we were such good friends in college, I think people figured I'd been pining for her all that time. Kara and I talked all of two minutes about how nice it was to be left alone because of peoples' mistake about our relationship. We decided we should just let them go on believing it. After that, we just behaved as we always did, and let other people make up the rest."

"And what about now?" Aidan asked, his voice so tentative it made Ethan's heart break. The man turned his head and stared out the window, breaking eye contact. A small tremor rocked through Aidan, but Ethan knew it didn't have anything to do with the early spring chill that still existed outside. Aidan touched his fingers to the glass, looking as if he wanted to reach through it to the dense copse of trees on the other side. "I want to be there for you at the funeral tomorrow, more than anything in the world. But I don't want to embarrass you or Wyn, and I don't want to turn your mother's funeral into a spectacle or a joke. She was too special for that, and I love you too much to give you another thing to stress about during such a difficult time." Aidan's chest rose and fell in a rough wave, and his fingers closed into a tight fist against the window. "Damn it, maybe I shouldn't have come to you today and stirred stuff up. Maybe I should have waited until you've had some time to heal."

Aidan's face reflected in the glass. The uncertainty within spoke volumes through his dewy gaze, and it fisted Ethan in the chest. "Hey, hey, don't say that." He drew Aidan against him, and then lowered them both until they were lying on their sides facing the window, with Aidan tucked in tight against Ethan's front. Ethan held Aidan around his stomach, and rested his chin on Aidan's shoulder. Staring out into the thick woods where they had become real friends, first kissed, and declared their love, Ethan whispered, his voice thick, "The very fact that I'm burying someone I love tomorrow proves how little time we have in this life. We've already wasted an awful lot of it due to other peoples' prejudices, our own fears and anger, and just in general getting into a pattern of living apart that we didn't know how to break. But you're home now, and we're together. If nothing else," he kissed the smooth, warm skin covering Aidan's shoulder, "I need my best friend with me when I say goodbye to my mom tomorrow." Ethan found Aidan's hand and clutched it tightly. "You're the only thing getting me through this, and it's only going to get harder before it starts to get easier. I'm sorry I scared you when I ran off and left you without a word. My head was all over the place, but it's not anymore. At least, not in regard to you. I don't want to do this alone. Please don't make me."

"Oh, baby." Aidan rolled onto his back and pulled Ethan on top of him. "Shh, shh." He buried his hands in Ethan's hair and pressed a kiss to his cheek, his temple, then rested his lips against Ethan's forehead. "No matter what we show the world, I am never leaving you again. I'll be right there with you." He separated their faces, and they found each other's gaze, intense and bright. "If that's what you want."

"I do." Ethan's heart felt almost too full to bear it, and that somehow felt wrong, but at the same time, very, very right. "Mom would want you there too. I think she'll be smiling down at me -- on us -- happy that we finally forgave and got it right."

"Then that's where I'll be." Aidan held Ethan's face, his grip strong and sure, making Ethan feel safe and cherished. "At your side."

As Ethan looked into Aidan's eyes, he brushed his fingers over the sharp planes of Aidan's face, learning the new lines and angles, updating the picture of the eighteen-year-old boy he had loved so long ago. "I love you, you know."

"You are my heart, Ash." Aidan pulled Ethan to him for a clinging, fast, raw kiss. He broke the connection, turned their faces until their cheeks melded, and they stared out into the trees. After a long moment, he whispered roughly, "You always were."

Ethan felt the truth of Aidan's words sink into his pores, causing a tremor when they found and took root in Ethan's heart. "You're mine too."

Their fingers entwined, Aidan brought Ethan's hand to his lips and kissed the back. "Good to know." Their gazes met in the reflection of the glass. "Good to know."

With the shadows of the tall trees creating patterns over their bodies, Ethan settled into Aidan's embrace and closed his eyes, secure in the arms of his lover and best friend.

EPILOGUE

"Ah fuck, Ash…" Aidan gritted his teeth against the new pleasure Ethan wreaked in his ass. Ethan kissed and flicked his tongue over Aidan's hole, sucking and relaxing the muscle, but making Aidan's cock rock-hard and, at the same time, needy and leaking a river of precum. Ethan had been working Aidan's channel over with the steady thrust of three fingers for long minutes already, and Aidan ached for Ethan to fuck him. "Too good, baby, too good." He rolled his hips and pushed back, reaching for more. He curled his hands into fists, pressing with all of his might into the window. "Too much. Gonna make me come."

Ethan pulled off his task for a moment and took a bite out of Aidan's left buttock, making him yelp. "You can take it,

Morgan." He smacked Aidan with the flat of his palm, rushing blood to Aidan's butt cheek. "Just keep bracing yourself against the window, and don't touch your dick."

With that, Ethan pushed with one pointed spear of his tongue, straight into Aidan's ass.

"Ahhh shit, shit…" Aidan howled with pleasure, which just seemed to spur Ethan on to lick and forage, somehow making this new kind of kiss deeper and more intimate, and blowing Aidan's mind. They'd never done this before, and truthfully, Aidan didn't know how much more he could take before he exploded his release all over the glass of the picture window.

Gasping, Aidan tried to breathe and focus on something other than the joy Ethan pulled from his body with every touch. He bit the inside of his cheek and stared at the picture he made in the reflection of the window, his face a shadowed haze of desire and lust, his pupils pinpoints, and his chest rising and falling in big waves with every erratic breath he took. His cock stuck out big and hard, pointing north, as if it reached for a hand that it had thus far been denied. He had his legs spread shoulder width apart, and he leaned slightly forward, straight-arming the window in order to remain upright. But with every rimming and deep lick Ethan delivered to his ass, Aidan slipped a little bit closer to the edge.

"Ash, Ash," Aidan begged, no longer caring about anything except getting Ethan inside him so that he could come. "Please. I need you. Oh Christ." His prick was so damn hard it hurt. "Fuck me. Please."

Ethan reared up and plunged inside Aidan. In one thrust, he filled Aidan with unbearable joy as he took Aidan's ass to the hilt.

"Ohhh fuck!" Aidan cried out at the wonderful stretch and burn of Ethan's taking, his channel clutching and squeezing Ethan's cock for more.

Ethan covered Aidan completely from behind. He stretched his arms out right along Aidan's, weaving their fingers against the glass. Tucking his chin over Aidan's shoulder, Ethan fanned hot, moist breath against Aidan's heated skin. Finally, *fucking finally*, he started to pump his hips and move his length in and out of Aidan's ass. Their gazes found one another in the reflection, and the intensity in Ethan's blue eyes snared Aidan just as completely as did his body.

"So beautiful." The whispered words from Ethan slipped into Aidan's ear and snaked all the way through his body, causing a shiver. "You're so fucking beautiful."

Aidan turned his head and captured Ethan's mouth in a hard kiss, forcing his way inside with an aggressive thrust of his tongue. Moaning, Ethan licked and bit right back. At the same time, he dropped one hand to Aidan's cock and wrapped it up in a vise-like hold. Aidan bucked into Ethan's fist, his cock screaming for release.

"Come for me, baby." Ethan stroked Aidan's turgid length as he gave permission. "Come right now." He claimed another hard, bruising kiss.

Aidan couldn't help but obey. He came in a fast, furious

flood. "Ahh… Ahh … fuck yeeeess…" He moaned low, spraying the picture window with thick streaks of seed. He fused his forehead to Ethan's as it happened, just as his channel contracted tightly around Ethan's cock, the length still buried deep inside Aidan's body.

Ethan made a choking sound. He jammed his hips forward, groaning as his cock swelled within Aidan and stretched his walls, pushing another spit of cum out of Aidan's body. Orgasm hit Ethan hard, jerking him against the back of Aidan, and then warming Aidan inside with the wet heat of Ethan's release.

They stood there attached to each other for a prolonged moment, almost supporting each other, as they regained their strength and breathing.

Finally recovered, Aidan chuckled. He opened his eyes and found Ethan waiting for him. "Damn, Ash." He paused, gasping through a last streak of pleasure as Ethan withdrew his cock and stepped back. "You worked me over good." Heat rushed through Aidan's body as he relived Ethan down on his knees behind him, *learning* him in a new way. "Never knew you wanted to do something like that before."

"Been thinking about it for a lot of years, just like everything else we're discovering and doing." Ethan slid his arm around Aidan's waist and pecked a kiss high on his cheek. "Besides, I figured if you could handle that without cracking, then you can stand up to just about anything we face today, without losing your cool."

A month had gone by since Ethan's mother passed away,

and while the men had openly renewed their friendship in public, they hadn't really done anything that would give too much cause for speculation.

Today, that would change.

Aidan lifted his hand and caressed Ethan's jaw. "You sure you're ready?" He knew Ethan still grieved, and he didn't want to add to the man's burden. When they were officially out, people would stare, whisper behind their backs, and they might even have to battle to keep their jobs. "We will do this on your timetable. You just say the word."

Ethan took Aidan's hand and kissed the palm. "I'm ready. Let's clean this mess up," he eyed the residue drying on the window, "take a shower, and hit the firehouse. Okay?"

Aidan took in the handsomeness of this mussed, blond god of a man, and smiled through the rush of love that hit him. "Okay. But you made that happen," he pointed at the streaky glass, "so you clean it up."

He ran for the bathroom, Ethan hot on his heels.

———

"So, YOU ALL ARE OUR colleagues and friends, and we thought you should know first." Aidan swept his gaze over every firefighter on his crew, both full-time and volunteer, making steady eye contact with every member of his staff. "We don't intend to either flaunt nor apologize for our relationship," his heart skittered as Ethan slipped his hand into Aidan's just then, "but rather than have everyone rampant with speculation, we thought we'd just be open about the fact that we are together.

"I haven't been at this job long," Aidan went on, "but I've loved it from the first moment I came on board. I don't intend to give it up, so just in case there's a fight or push from the folks who hired me to edge me out, you all need to know I will fight that possibility and don't intend to leave. I hope you all feel you can continue to respect me as your chief, but if you can't, don't think you're going to sit quietly until I'm gone. I'm not going anywhere without one hell of a knock-down, drag-out fight."

"I know I'm only volunteer crew," Ethan added, "but that all goes the same for me. I won't be pushed out."

Devlin stepped forward, his eyes a tough, flat silver, and his arms crossed against his chest. "If they force you guys out they'll find out I'm gay, and lose me too."

Aidan's heart stopped as his brother outed himself in support of him and Ethan. *Christ.*

Kara moved to Devlin's side and linked her arm in his. "I guess they would lose me too, since I'm a lesbian."

"Yeah." Pete, with his gray hair and ebony skin, slung his arm around Devlin, declaring, "I'm gay too."

Coop took a big step forward, locking himself in a military stance. "I don't know, I think I might like guys too, so they'd lose their biggest guy on the volunteer crew."

Marcus stepped up next, and one by one, everyone on staff proclaimed to be gay and would no longer work at the firehouse if Aidan lost his job.

Devlin sputtered, "B-but I'm not just supporting my

brother. I really am gay."

"Hell, son," Pete gave Devlin a noogie, "sure you are. We all are. I'm as gay as the day is long." All humor suddenly left Pete's eyes and demeanor. "I'm whatever I need to be to stand up for what's right, and what's right is that no one loses a job they are qualified to do just because of someone else's prejudices. Nothing else needs to be said about it."

More murmurs of agreement went up from the crowd.

Devlin turned and looked at Aidan. "They don't understand."

Aidan held up his hand, stopping Devlin. "Don't worry about it right now. I appreciate what you did." He brought his fingers to his lips and delivered a sharp whistle, quieting everyone down. "I thank you for your support, and I appreciate your faith in me."

"Forgive me, Chief," Coop said, "but I've gotta be honest and say that it's not so much you I openly support as it is Ethan. I hardly know you, but I've known Ethan for seven years. I know he's a good man who hasn't ever let down our friendship or walked away from someone who needed help."

Aidan watched everyone in the group nod in agreement, and his chest swelled with pride in the man he loved.

"You're getting the benefit of our trust in Ethan, sir," Coop shared. "I'm willing to go to bat for you because of him. I don't think he would make a bad choice and fall for someone who wasn't a stand-up guy, so I'm taking a leap of faith that you are deserving of my support too. Pardon me for saying so," his dark eyes turned downright fierce, "but don't let him down, or us. If you do, this crew could become a very different kind of mob."

"Understood." Aidan might have taken offense or been hurt if he weren't so damn happy to see so many people in Ethan's corner. Hell, he could understand that, he had been there first, thirteen years ago. "I'm still the probie here, but I promise you that I will pass the test. Both with Ethan," he drew the man in question against his chest, "and as your chief."

Coop gave a curt nod. "That's all I needed to hear."

"Pizza!" A familiar delivery boy appeared in the open garage door, boxes full of fragrant pies stacked high. *Ahh, my back-up plan has arrived.* Bribery. Thank God Aidan hadn't needed it. All he'd ever needed was Ethan.

Aidan palmed a handful of twenties out of his pocket, passed them to Devlin with one hand, and turned Ethan in his embrace with the other. The man's face flamed, but his eyes sparkled brightly, warming Aidan's already heated heart.

"If I wasn't already completely in love with you," Aidan locked his hands at the small of Ethan's back and held him close, "their devotion to you would have had me there in a flash."

"Don't let Coop's gruffness fool you." Ethan circled his arms around Aidan's neck and pulled their faces to almost touching. "They all respect you immensely already, or you wouldn't have had a complete turnout for this meeting. They've transferred their loyalty to you, and they listen when you speak. They all want to be good firefighters for you."

"I want to be as good a man." Aidan's voice caught, roughening with emotion he could no longer hide. "For you."

"You are." Ethan spoke without hesitation, his gaze never wavering. "You always were."

"Thank you." Aidan lowered his head and brushed his lips against Ethan's with a slow, easy kiss. A couple of whistles and catcalls rose up from the crowd. Aidan only smiled, teased the tip of his tongue through Ethan's seam, and licked, sparking their particular flame.

Aidan would never run from Ethan's fire again.

THE END

ABOUT THE AUTHOR

I am an air force brat and spent most of my growing up years living overseas in Italy and England, as well as Florida, Georgia, Ohio, and Virginia while we were stateside. I now live in Florida once again with my big, wonderfully pushy family and my three-legged cat, Harry. I have been reading romance novels since I was twelve years old, and twenty-five years later I still adore them. Currently, I have an unexplainable obsession with hockey goaltenders, and an unabashed affection for *The Daily Show* with Jon Stewart.

Devlin & Garrick
A SEEKING REDEMPTION BOOK

Currently available in e-book format from Liquid Silver Books
Available in Print in August 2011

PROLOGUE

"If you sit there in silence for one more second, I'm going to assume that you fucked him."

Devlin Morgan jerked out of his daydreaming and landed a narrow-eyed glare on the young woman sitting across from him. The words "you fucked him" had registered in his head -- *in his little sister's voice* -- and dragged Devlin back to reality with a shudder. He did not talk about sex with his sister. Especially not in the middle of a diner during lunch hour.

Especially when you're not having any, Devlin added to himself silently.

Maddie smirked at Devlin from the other side of the booth. She pushed her long dark hair behind her ears. "Yep, I thought that would get your attention." Light gray eyes that matched

214 | CAMERON DANE

his twinkled with laughter one second and then softened in the next. "I'd say you're allowed to brood and keep quiet all you want, except you're the one who invited me to lunch."

"I was getting a little stir crazy sitting around the apartment," Devlin answered. "I hate that I can't go back to work yet." In performing his duties as a firefighter, Devlin had injured himself while carrying a man out of an apartment building. One month of rehabbing his leg and lower back now under his belt, he still had a few more weeks before he could get back on the job. "I have PT in a few hours but I needed a change of scenery before I started rearranging the walls with my bare hands."

"Ahh." Maddie nodded, but pursed her lips and gave him the stink eye at the same time. "And here I thought you might finally want to talk about your date."

Darren. The guy was one of only a very few openly gay men in Redemption that Devlin wasn't related to by blood or civil ceremony. The two he claimed as kin were Aidan and Ethan. Aidan was Devlin's brother and Ethan was Aidan's partner. Disgustingly happy as a couple for three years now, they made forever look attainable and inviting. Devlin loved hanging out with them, but the twist of envy that came with seeing them in a successful partnership drove home exactly how far away he was from finding someone himself.

He just couldn't get excited about Darren, though. When Devlin thought about what Aidan and Ethan had, a longing for the same constricted his chest, and he couldn't hold back the memories of looking into bottomless green eyes, of gripping thick, wide shoulders, and of gasping for breath the first time another man sank his cock deep into Devlin's virgin ass.

Stop it! Devlin slammed closed a thick metal door on the rest of that picture. *Gradyn is long out of your life. For good.*

"Earth to Dev." Maddie snapped her fingers in Devlin's face and yanked him back to the diner again. "Don't make me say the word fuck again."

Devlin shot his sister another pointed glare. "You just did."

"So you hadn't drifted that far away this time," Maddie said as the devil came back into her eyes. "In that case... Your second date with cutie Darren. When is it going to happen?"

Incessant chatter from his first date with Darren still rang in Devlin's ears. "We have something set up for tomorrow night, but I think I'm going to cancel it."

"Really?" Maddie sat up straighter. "He's attractive and I always remember him being a sweetie in school. What's not working for you?"

Maybe that was part of the problem with Darren. His age. Maddie could remember him being a sweet kid because she actually went through high school with Darren not that long ago. Devlin opened his mouth to say so when a shadow crossed their table.

"Maddie." An older gentleman Devlin recognized as a member of the city council paused at their table. "Just the girl I was hoping to find." The man then smoothly transitioned his attention to Devlin and stuck out his hand. "Hi there. Larry

Courtland. And you're Devlin. Correct? How's the physical therapy coming along?"

Devlin had never met this guy in person but figured he must have read about Devlin's injuries in the newspaper a while back. "I'm fine, sir." He shook the guy's hand. "I should be back at the firehouse in a couple of weeks."

"Good. Very good." Larry slipped his hands into his pockets and rocked back on his heels. "The council was speaking with your brother very recently about increasing the budget for the fire department. One of the hardships Chief Morgan cited was when his paid staff gets injured and puts you all down a man."

"It's tough, sir." Aidan was not only Devlin's brother, but also his boss. "We could use a couple more full-time people at the house."

Maddie touched Larry Courtland's elbow and deftly brought his attention back to her. "Did you need me for something, Mr. Courtland?"

"I went by the garage and that new guy told me you were here." With his hands still in his pockets, Larry leaned close to Maddie, as if imparting a state secret. "My baby has a funny hum, and you're the only one I trust to treat her right."

"Ahh." Maddie nodded, and her eyes lit up as she tapped her fingers against her lips. "Do you have her with you right now?"

"Right there." Mr. Courtland pointed, and Devlin followed the line of his finger through the window to a cherry-red classic corvette in the parking lot.

"How's your schedule?" Maddie asked, clearly comfortable as hell, and making Devlin all kinds of proud. His sister was one hell of a mechanic. "Do you have time for me to go take a quick listen right now?" She pulled her hair back into a ponytail and slid out of the booth before the man answered.

"That's why I came in." Mr. Cortland put his hand at the small of her back and gestured toward the exit. "Ladies first."

"Be right back, Dev." Maddie squeezed his shoulder as she walked past. "Knock on the window if our food arrives."

"No problem," he told her, but she was already out the door.

As Devlin watched Maddie cross the parking lot to the corvette, he let his mind wander back to his date with Darren. Compact and wiry, with sandy-colored hair, a mouth that ran a mile a minute, and hands that gestured just as fast, Darren brought to Devlin's mind pictures of chipmunks gathering nuts for winter at a furious rate. That image had popped into Dev's head over pasta during their first date, and once there, he could not shake it.

Darren. Darren. Darren. Why don't I want you?

The guy was harmless. He really did seem nice enough. God knew he had pretty blue eyes and a full lower lip that should have Devlin wanting to pull it between his teeth and find his way into that mouth for a deep kiss. Devlin just knew Darren's body kicked ass too; he didn't have to see it naked to get a real good sense of its rock-solid shape beneath the too-snug shirts and jeans he often wore.

Everything about Darren should be right, even for just a no-strings tryst, but Devlin couldn't forget another fling, one that left all others pale in comparison before they even happened…

———

…*Oh God. This is not me. I shouldn't be here.*

Devlin kept his head down and nursed his watered-down beer while techno music blasted in the background and a dozen or so young men gyrated some twenty feet away on a dance floor. An equally small group of guys littered the long line of the bar, although most of them had their backs to the wood. They openly admired the view of dancers swaying so closely together Devlin wondered if a group orgy might break out right in front of him. Then he figured the club likely paid the hot dancing men to do exactly what they were doing, and that soon a whole lot more customers would trickle in and spend too much money on cheap drinks so they could stare, hope, and maybe even join in the fun, just like Devlin was supposed to be doing himself.

Except, it all felt so impersonal, and Devlin suddenly didn't think he had anything to prove. He was gay. He had wet dreams about random and not-so-random men on a nightly basis and had been noticing masculine bodies and male smells since he'd hit puberty. Just because he'd recently turned twenty-three and still hadn't experienced actual full-on sex with another man didn't mean he had to put-up or shut-up and go straight.

Devlin groaned into his drink. Nearly a thousand bucks on

a round-trip plane ticket, spending money, and a motel for a long weekend in San Francisco, and *now* he had the realization that he should have just stayed home?

Real smart, Dev. You're building yourself a nice track record of leaping before you look.

At least now he knew anonymous sex wasn't his thing. And he felt less guilty for booking the cheap motel rather than the expensive hotel. If it was just going to be him, he didn't need anything fancy. Devlin went ahead and decided he wouldn't spend a whole lot of time in the room anyway. This city had plenty of sights to see that didn't have a damned thing to do with hooking up with men. The trip wouldn't be a waste of his hard-earned money. He could do a hundred touristy things before he had to head home to Maine.

Might as well start now.

"Excuse me." Devlin signaled the bartender before the guy stepped away and strutted his amazing ass down the bar for someone else. The stud looked up at him, and Devlin said, "Can I go ahead and pay my tab please?"

As soon as Devlin got a nod, heat from another source rode his back, drawing a shiver down his spine. Then a voice as smooth as expensive bourbon sank into his ear. "I wondered how long it would take you to ask for the check."

The towering muscular body that went with the deep, rich voice slipped in between the barstools and leaned against the empty one next to Devlin.

"You don't look like you belong here, beautiful," the man

said. He looked right at Devlin and nearly stopped Devlin's heart.

Devlin opened his mouth and was surprised his voice didn't come out as a croak. "Neither do you."

Holy shit. That was the understatement of the year. The man wore a leather jacket with a white T-shirt beneath, faded jeans, and biker boots, but that wasn't exactly what had Devlin swallowing funny. *Not even close.* Indigo colored tattoos that looked almost tribal in design covered part of this man's smooth, bald scalp and went down to a corner of his forehead, around his left eye, over part of his cheek, and down his jaw line to his neck, where the pattern disappeared under his shirt.

"You're right. I don't belong here." The guy answered Devlin's question, drawing Devlin's attention to his sensuous mouth.

The bartender came up right then and slid a credit card receipt and pen in front of Devlin. Devlin added a tip and signed. All the while, every molecule in his being snapped to life and shot to the parts of his body closest to the tattooed man leaning next to him.

Devlin handed the signed receipt back to the bartender with a murmured "Thank you." He said another prayer of thanks when his hands stayed steady. God knew the rest of him shook inside.

"So." The tattooed man stayed on his barstool, allowing Devlin plenty of running room. Fuck, though, his pure green eyes held Devlin captive and made him feel stripped bare right in this techno club. "Do you want to get out of here?" That rich voice slipped into Devlin and infected his blood. "With me?"

"Yeah," Devlin automatically answered. *What the fuck is wrong with me?* Devlin darted his tongue out and wet the edge of his lip as his nerves skittered into overdrive. "I think I do."

The man dropped his focus to Devlin's mouth. It stayed there as he stood and moved in close. He curled his hand around Devlin's neck, pulled him in, and licked right over where Devlin had just dipped his tongue. Devlin jerked; the small contact shot tingles all the way through his body and moved quickly into his jeans. The guy's fingers dug into Devlin's nape right before he murmured a curse and licked Devlin's mouth again, this time drawing a needful little noise of out of Devlin he could not control.

"Damn it." The man's voice suddenly thicker, he let go of Devlin's neck and grabbed his hand. "We have to get out of here right now. Let's go."

"Wait!" Flashing red lights signaled in Devlin's mind, and he tugged against the bigger man's vise-tight hold on his hand. When the guy looked back, Devlin said, "I don't even know your name."

The man smiled, and it went all the way up to his eyes. He let up his death grip on Devlin's hand, and instead threaded their fingers together in a gentler, but no less sure, hold. "Gradyn Connell. My mom and my sister call me Denny, and most everybody else calls me GC. What's yours?"

"Devlin Morgan." Devlin grinned back. Couldn't seem to

rein it in. "Some people shorten it to Dev. Doesn't bother me one way or the other."

"Okay, *Devlin*, now we know a little something about each other." Gradyn looked down at their linked hands and then came back up to Devlin's eyes. "Or have you changed your mind about leaving with me?"

"No." *Oh God. This is possibly the stupidest thing I've ever done.* Risky-crazy-stupid or not, something in Gradyn Connell's eyes made everything else that was a little bit scary about him disappear. That green gaze of this man, that didn't waver, kept Devlin's hand firmly in Gradyn's hold when every bit of intelligence he possessed told him this was a bad idea. "I want to go with you."

Gradyn smiled even bigger. Without another word, he pulled Devlin toward the exit.

This time, Devlin didn't fight it…

———

…"Do I have to say that word again?" Maddie whispered in a diabolical tone at Devlin's ear, drawing him away from memories of someone he'd repeatedly promised himself he wouldn't waste time thinking about anymore.

Five years, Dev. Time to forget that weekend ever happened.

Ignoring Maddie's threat, and shaking off his own disturbing thoughts, Devlin asked, "Did you figure out the problem with Mr. Courtland's car?"

"It's not something I can fix in a parking lot. He doesn't

have time to drive it back out to the garage." Maddie dangled a set of car keys off one finger, and Devlin would have thought she twirled a diamond ring. "So he left it for me."

Devlin chuckled as he took another glance at the sweet ride outside. "You have the coolest job."

"Yeah," a little smile added to the life shining in his sister's eyes, "I kind of do. I'm going to need you to drive my truck back to the garage, okay?" Maddie had done the driving, and Devlin's car was back at her work.

He snatched the corvette keys out of her hand and held them above his head. "Why don't I drive the 'vette and you drive your truck?"

Maddie surged up from the booth and grabbed the keys right back with a whip-fast move. She smirked for a second but quickly sobered and pocketed the keys. "Mr. Courtland has a heavy foot and hand, and that makes his car very temperamental to handle. You just got the okay to drive again. I don't need it pulling on you, and you driving it off the road. I'm thinking about your safety more than the fact that it wouldn't be professional of me to let you drive it."

"Fine." Four weeks of limitations and no job to rely on as an outlet turned Devlin's tone somewhat surly. "But don't be surprised if you go to watch last week's *True Blood* and it's mysteriously gone from the DVR."

Maddie snorted and rolled her eyes. "Fat chance. You love that show too much to delete one just to spite me."

"Maybe I've already watched it," he shot back.

"You wouldn't." She didn't even flinch. "Not without me."

That was true. Pathetic and sad, but true. They shared an apartment, and neither one of them dated enough to disrupt any of their routines.

Their waitress breezed to the table right then, just long enough to deposit two plates of greasy food in front of Devlin and Maddie. She offered a quick "Enjoy" before moving on to the next group of customers entering the diner.

"Yeah, all right," Devlin muttered as he picked up his bacon cheeseburger. "Shut up and eat your food."

Maddie flashed him a fast smile and dug into her mile-high club sandwich.

———

"YOU SHOULD AT LEAST CONSIDER giving Darren another shot," Maddie said as she joined Devlin next to his car in the parking lot of Corsini's Garage. "I don't remember him being a chatterbox. Maybe you're not doing enough talking and he feels like he has to fill in the awkward silences on his own."

Devlin rolled his eyes. His sister had picked up their conversation from the diner as if she and Devlin hadn't driven across town in separate vehicles.

"I'm going to go now, Maddie." Devlin looked at her from over the hood of his piece of crap Corolla that Maddie kept alive with duct tape and prayer, and delivered a look that matched the firmness in his tone. "I'll see you at home tonight."

"No, wait! Come inside with me for a second. I want to

show you something."

"What now?" Devlin didn't move. "I have to get to the hospital for my therapy session."

"You have a few minutes," she answered in a knowing voice. "It's something you might want to consider buying when I'm done restoring it." She sing-songed the information like the Pied Piper from over her shoulder, and Devlin could not ignore the enticing tune.

Devlin jogged and caught up to her side. "What is it?" She knew he hated his car but that he also refused to sink a pile of money into something new that wasn't truly special.

"Just a '77 Trans Am that will have all the interior specs and gleam with shiny black paint and the Pontiac Firebird insignia on the hood by the time I'm done with it."

Shit. "Really?" Devlin used to watch a certain movie over and over when he was a kid, and he had latched onto wanting the damned car like nobody's business.

"Really," Maddie answered. She pushed open the side door to the garage and Devlin followed her inside the big, cavernous building. "It doesn't look like much right now, but give us some time in between the jobs that pay the bills and Garrick and I will have it looking and running better than the original. Follow me." She circled around two cars. "We have it curtained off and under canvas in back."

They rounded the front end of an Accord and came across a pair of long legs encased in Corsini's standard blue coveralls sticking out from under the car.

"Ooh, stay still, G." Maddie tapped her boot against the boot of the guy under the car. "I think I remember the words to a double-dutch game I used to play when I was a kid." Maddie proceeded to skip in a pattern over and between the man's spread legs, all the while singing an old jump-roping song. At the end, she jumped a foot away with a grand "Ta-da! I did it."

A chuckle drifted out from under the car, followed by a smooth, deep voice. "If you're done skipping rope with my legs, Maddie, can you get me a new light? This one just died."

Holy shit. Devlin trembled as the rich tone of that damned voice washed over his flesh. He knew that voice all the way down to his soul.

Devlin planted his hand against the hood of the Accord so he didn't stumble.

He couldn't fucking believe it.

"Gradyn?" This time his voice did croak. …

Made in the USA
Lexington, KY
06 November 2011